THE BEST OF

GAUNTLET

EXPLORING THE LIMITS OF FREE EXPRESSION

A RICHARD KASAK BOOK

THE BEST OF GAUNTLET

EXPLORING THE LIMITS OF FREE EXPRESSION

EDITED BY BARRY HOFFMAN

The following have been reprinted with permission of the author from *Gauntlet*.

"Stephen King Special" Volume No. 2, 1991

Bullwhips, Sex Slaves, and *Catcher in the Rye*; *Hot Box*: Wrong Time, Wrong Place; *Raw*: An Interview with Art Spiegelman; The Victim's Side; The Art of Homophobia.

"Media Manipulation" Volume No. 4, 1992

Hate and the Art of Queer Media Spins; Still Lurking in the Shadows After All These Years; *Cherry*, Me and Censorship.

"Black Racism" Volume No. 6, 1993

The Sting of Pornography; "Boiled" Diana; The Missing Demand in the Gay Agenda; True Perversion; The Erotic Eleven; Nude, Fucked, and Freezing; *On Our Backs* Gets Kicked in the Ass.

"Politically (In)correct" Volume No. 3, 1992

The Shameful Enforcement of Video Chastity; Finding the Cost of Freedom; An Interview with Joe Coleman; San Francisco v. *Basic Instinct*; Cheri Gaulke: Performance Artist Under Attack.

"Porn in the USA" Volume No. 5, 1993

An Interview with Annie Sprinkle; Above the Law: The Justice Department's War Against the First Amendment; The Mastur Race: An Interview with Dian Hanson; Pornography's Victims; Sex, Smears, and Feminists; The Arguments Against Pornography; An Interview with Candida Royalle.

"In Defense of Prostitution" Volume No. 7, 1994

Whoring in Utopia.

First Richard Kasak Book Edition 1994
First printing August 1994
ISBN 1-56333-202-7

Cover Art © Brian Lynch
Cover Design by Kurt Griffith

Manufactured in the United States of America
Published by Masquerade Books, Inc.
801 Second Avenue
New York, N.Y. 10017

THE BEST OF

GAUNTLET

EXPLORING THE LIMITS OF FREE EXPRESSION

INTRODUCTION

A *Best of Gauntlet*? Five years creeps up on one, but here we are with seven issues under our belt, and I recall an early review from *Screw* praising our premier issue, but wondering if there'd be a second. We've beat the odds thanks to some wonderful writers, loyal subscribers and distributors who've kept faith in us.

Why *Gauntlet*? I've circumvented the question many a time, as it applies directly to my day job, and it's that job that allowed me to start *Gauntlet*. It's time to let the cat out of the bag, however, and stop beating around the bush. As a teacher I've experienced censorship...personally. I'd authored plays at my school for five years (award-winning, SRO affairs). I wrote the scripts, a professional composer wrote the music and my students penned lyrics for the songs. I *never* had one parent whose student was in a ply complain about the subject matter or content. Plays focused on graffiti, the homeless, and loneliness among others. My final play dealt with teenage runaways. One of the bigwigs at the school (whose child was in no way part of the production) felt the topic too sensitive, and had the ear of my principal. For the first time he demanded approval of the script, and literally line-edited the sucker. A short scene where a father ripped off his daughter's necklace because he felt she was growing up too fast (based on an actual experience of one of my students) was too violent and cut. The dialogue of a blue-collar father was deemed "black" and I was told to write it grammatically correct. In actuality the character was based on a white custodian; the focus was on class *not* race. A song dealing with the death of runaways had to be altered at the last minute (lyrics composed by students, remember). AIDS spread through unsafe sex (*sex* being the operative word here) was out. The word butt (I was "sensitive" not to have my students use the word "ass") was given a swift kick. And there was more. The final presentation was a bastardized version of the original, but that was not the final act of censorship. That was to be more insidious. I was not asked to write a script the next year—now that's censorship of the highest order. A few parents (aka a special interest group) decided the fate of sixty student performers and, in the final analysis, of a successful educational program.

Thus, *Gauntlet* was born; my outlet to expose hypocrites who want to shut up those who may hold unpopular beliefs.

Gauntlet's purpose is to stimulate debate. We don't preach to the already converted. We provoke first amendment purists by tackling thorny issues that fall into gray areas of limits of free expression. And we present both sides of issues. We challenge readers with differing viewpoints and allow the reader to make an informed decision. We respect our readers, so we have no problem allowing the "opposition" space. Moreover, one must know one's enemies arguments in order to rebut them. Finally, *Gauntlet* is founded on the principle of providing the reader with the material that's been deemed offensive. We won't run a story if we can't get permission to print the censored art. It keeps us out of Waldenbooks, but allows me to live with myself. *Gauntlet* was born of censorship, and as long as I'm at the helm I won't censor its pages for greater distribution.

What follows is a *Gauntlet* sampler. It's the best of *Gauntlet*'s pieces dealing with sex and gay/lesbian issues, but we've also covered political correctness, black racism and much more.

Gauntlet is published each May and November. Pick up a copy, because the definitive "best" of Gauntlet may not yet have been written.

Enough already. Read, enjoy and be prepared to find something that will probably offend you.

—Barry Hoffman, Editor
Gauntlet
309 Powell Road
Springfield, PA 19064

THE BEST OF

GAUNTLET

EXPLORING THE LIMITS OF FREE EXPRESSION

THE STING OF PORNOGRAPHY

Cecil E. Greek, Ph.D.

Both U.S. Customs and the U.S. Postal Inspection Service initiated major sting operations, such as Operation Looking Glass, in the late 1980s, aimed principally at catching those who are inclined to purchase child pornography. The government used a variety of questionable techniques which bordered on entrapment to locate potential customers [Stanley, 1989:323; *W. 57th*, 1988; Howard, 1992].

In 1992 the U.S. Supreme Court ruled in a case involving entrapment in these sting operations [*Jacobson* v. *U.S.*]. Keith Jacobson, a Nebraska farmer, was targeted by the U.S. Postal Inspection Service's Operation Looking Glass because his name was found on a list of customers who previously had purchased nude magazines which included nude pictures of boys. As a result, the government spent two and one-half years attempting to entice Mr. Jacobson to purchase illegal child pornography.

No efforts were first made to find out whether Mr. Jacobson—or any of the other targeted individuals—were indeed child molesters. According to Chief Postal Inspector Daniel Mahalco, since the distributors of pornography had all been driven out of the business, the next step was to go after the consumers of such materials, with the ultimate hope that children would now be protected from sexual abuse and molestation [Howard, 1992] Mahalco reported that of the 160 people indicted as a result of Operation Looking Glass, 35 cases of sexual molestation were uncovered. In targeting suspects, the Postal Inspection Service presumed that previous purchase of nude pictures of children was sufficient to prove criminal predisposition to purchase illegal child pornography, which they assumed was collected only by practicing pedophiles. When asked why he had not first checked to find out whether Jacobson was a pedophile, Mahalco replied, "We're not going to wait until someone molest a child before we go after him" [Howard, 1992].

The tactics employed against Jacobson were similar to those used against hundreds of other unsuspecting individuals. First, Jacobson was sent a series of letters from a phony organization, the American Hedonist Society (others employed by the sting included "Research Facts," "Midlands Data Research," "Freedom's Choice," and "Ohio Valley Action League [Stanley, 1989:323]), claiming to be a First Amendment sexual libertarian group out to stop government censorship. Targeted individuals who responded to the mailing were sent questionnaires and surveys regarding their interests. For example, Heartland Institute for a New Tomorrow sent Jacobson a survey, claiming it was trying to gauge the public's interest in the repeal of all statutes regarding nonviolent sexual activities, including the removal of age limitations. In addition, HINT claimed to be involved in lobbying efforts and hoped to interest Jacobson in purchasing fund-raising items from a forthcoming catalog, hinting that porn might be available.

People who returned the surveys were then offered pen pals

who shared their interests. While Jacobson never responded to the pen pal request, a number of other men did. Those who did were given pen pals. Sometimes male postal inspectors pretended to be young, sexually adventurous, recently divorced or widowed mothers who hinted that they were looking for a relationship with an older man and that their children might be available for photographs. Some of the men became quite infatuated with these young women who seemed to be so interested in them, and lipstick-stained letters were not uncommon. Postal inspectors also pretended to be the young daughters of "sexually liberated" mothers who wanted to ask their new special "uncle" intimate questions about sex. In general, the phony letters employed a technique known as "mirroring," with the postal/customs agents attempting to reflect whatever the interests were of the persons they had contacted.

Sometimes pen pals even offered to trade child pornography with the targeted individuals. After two-and-one-half years of such solicitations from both postal inspectors and the U.S. Customs Service's Operation Borderline, Jacobson, mostly out of curiosity, ordered a magazine containing child pornography from one of the catalogs offered by the Far East Trading Company. During this time period, the only such catalogs going through the mails were those of the government, the only known commercial outlet for such materials [Stanley, 1989]. When the magazine arrived at Jacobson's house he was arrested immediately; a search of his house found no other child pornography. He was later convicted and served his sentence. Five of the 160 indicted as a result of Operation Looking Glass committed suicide rather than face the embarrassment of public exposure. These included Robert Brase, Thomas Cleasby, Gary Hester, and Dale Riva.

A very interesting case was that of sixty-one-year-old Reverend John Zangger. He believed that circumcision was an unbiblical practice and devoted a considerable amount of time to speaking out against it. In order to demonstrate his belief, Zangger collected a series of slides from a research project which included photos of boys' uncircumcised penises and had these enlarged and transferred to videotape. In addition, he made a tape of himself masturbating his uncircumcised penis. With these tapes he hoped to demonstrate the superiority of uncircumcised penises. He shared these tapes with Postal Inspector Calvin Comfort, a.k.a. Jolene, a young woman who claimed she wanted to join his crusade against circumcision. In addition, Jolene feigned romantic interest in Zangger after watching his tape. Zangger then faced both child-pornography and adult-obscenity charges, was convicted of the former, but later had the conviction overturned [Swadey, 1993].

The Supreme Court had ruled in the Jacobson decision that the techniques described above as employed by the government constituted entrapment:

The government did not establish that the defendant, who had received mailings from the government purporting to be from organizations asserting individual rights, was predisposed to commit the offense prior to first contact by the government.... Government did not establish that the defendant had a predisposition, independent of government action, to receive child pornography through the mail where evidence showed that he was ready and willing to commit the offense only after government had engaged in two and one-half years of undercover activity consisting of communications from fictitious organizations and persons attempting to convince the defendant that he had the right or should have the right to engage in behavior proscribed by law [*Jacobson* v. *U.S.*, 1992:1535].

Nevertheless, the result of these increased efforts in the late 1980s was greater numbers of investigations, arrests, and convictions for child pornography. Arrests made by the Postal Inspector peaked at 314 in 1988.

While virtually no one would support the use of children in the making of pornographic photos or videos, little is actually known, despite the above arrest and conviction figures, about the extent of such practices in the contemporary United States. However, since the alleged dangers to children played such an important part in 1986 Meese Commission testimony and findings, it is not surprising that Congress also reacted to the Meese report by attempting to pass new legislation aimed at stiffening laws regarding child pornography, and that law enforcement officials stepped up their efforts in this area. In 1988, Congress passed the "Child Protection and Obscenity Enforcement Act." The bill's title is somewhat ironic, given that child pornography is not protected by the First Amendment [See *NY* v. *Ferber*, 1982; *Osborne* v. *Ohio*, 1990] and it is neither professionally manufactured nor sold commercially in the United States [Stanley, 1988]. (Child pornography is either imported from overseas or nonprofessionally produced by pedophiles who trade such materials with one another.) In reality, this bill was principally aimed at making sure that underaged performers, such as Traci Lords, are not allowed to pass themselves off as adults [National Obscenity Enforcement Unit, 1988:10-11]. To insure compliance, the law required proof that all the actors/models in a pornographic film or magazine were of legal age (18) at the time of the performance or photographing. The bill made the proof requirements retroactive, meaning that all photographs taken over the previous ten years, if they were still being commercially distributed, must have records to verify the ages of performers. The adult video industry's lobbying group (the Adult Video Association) joined with the mainstream publishing and film industries to oppose the bill, but it was passed anyway [Gree, 1989; Margold, 1989]. However, the bill was later found unconstitutional by the courts in 1989 [*American Library Association* v. *Thornburgh*] on the basis that the record-keeping provisions were too broad and overly burdensome, and posed a serious potential that persons not engaged in child pornography would be convicted [DeWitt, 1991:24]. In 1990, Congress reenacted the legislation, attempting to rectify the criticisms made in *American Library Association*. The revised law—The Child Protection Restoration and Penalties Enhancement Act—was also contested and struck down by a district court in Washington, D.C., in May 1992 on grounds similar to the first case.

The Child Protection and Obscenity Enforcement Act of 1988 was in fact the fourth piece of anti-pornography legislation passed by Congress since 1977, all enacted to eliminate child pornography—The Protection of Children Against Child Exploitation Act of 1977, The Child Protection Act of 1984, and The Child Sexual Abuse and Pornography Act of 1986 were the others [von Raab, 1986; Stanley, 1989:302]. A resulting paradox is that in a great many jurisdictions, teenagers have the full legal right to consent to sexual intercourse, but they may not legally consent to be photographed in a lascivious pose [Stanley, 1989:307]. Federal and state efforts at redefining what is "child pornography" have gone so far that many parents now fear taking nude pictures of their own children lest they be turned in by the photo processor, who is *not* required to report suspicious negatives [Andriette, 1991].

One of the most severe critics of the recent child porn campaigns is Lawrence Stanley. According to Stanley [1989:295], the production and commercial distribution of child pornography had been virtually eliminated when the first new federal law took effect in 1978, yet "kiddy porn" continued to be exploited nationwide by law enforcement officials, moral crusaders, politicians, and the media as a grave social danger. "Kiddy porn" was employed repeatedly as a rhetoric to justify new anti-pornography legislation in the 1980s [D'Emilio and Freedman, 1988:353]. Among the unsubstantiated claims made concerning pornographic exploitation of children were of: "child auctions in Amsterdam, toll-free numbers and mail-order houses for ordering child prostitutes, child 'snuff' films, satanic molestation rituals in which animals are dismembered, 'chains of American brothels and bordellos where children were kept under lock and key,' and motorcycle gang rapes" [Stanley, 1989:309]. A number of the unsubstantiated claims regarding child pornography by "child abuse experts" such as Judianne Densen-Gerber [1979, 1980] and Shirley O'Brien [1983] were uncritically accepted by the Meese Commission and included as fact in the report (See also [*NBC News*, 1985]). Alfred Regnery [1985:5], then head of OJJDP, made the outlandish claim that child pornography represented a one-half to one billion dollars a year industry.

In the early 1980s, the hysteria over child pornography merged with the "missing children" scare—which also later proved to be unfounded [Best, 1990]. In addition, claims about child pornography were sometimes attached to Fundamentalist legends regarding Satanism. A number of criminologists and sociologists of religion (Lyons [1988], Alexander Hicks [1991], Carlson and Larue [1989], Hicks [1991], Best [1990], and Richardson, et al [1991]) have argued that Christian fundamentalists—along with talk show hosts like Geraldo Rivera [1989]—have helped to give credence to a number of urban myths concerning a major upsurge in Satanic activity, including the following: young women—"breeders"—who are forced to give birth to hundreds of babies annually which are then sacrificed to Satan and cannibalized; daycare centers that covertly double as Satanic covens practicing ritualistic sexual abuse of children, including the production of child pornography; and a conspiracy of police, lawyers, judges and politicians hiding such practices from discovery. (For discussion of why right-wing Christians sometimes accept such conspiracy theories see Toch [1965:45–85] and Johnson [1983:163–186].) Judith Reisman [1991:133–136], for example, also claimed that ritualistic abuse and murder of children is advocated by magazines such as *Playboy*. She alleged that ten percent of *Playboy*'s cartoons feature killing, maiming, or murdering of children, thus linking pornography and Satanism. Reisman [1991:135] has also attacked the works of artists Robert Mapplethorpe and Andres Serrano as that of "satanic pornographers" and testified in the 1990 Cincinnati Mapplethorpe trial. No tapes, films, or photos produced by Satanic child-abusing rings and cults have ever been located [Stanley, 1988].

It was in this context that the Post Office designed their sting operation, yet another incidence of how law enforcement overreacts to public and political pressure to solve crime at all costs, including subverting the Constitution.

THE VICTIM'S SIDE: A FIRSTHAND ACCOUNT

Ron Leming

It's fine and dandy to spend a lifetime in endless discussions about the evils of child pornography; even to discuss whether it should, in some way, be permitted or tolerated. I'm all in favor of argument and discussion; but, in this particular argument, I feel that something is forgotten: the victim himself. You say you haven't forgotten? You say that's what this discussion is all about? *Bullshit*. The victim is not what the discussion is *about*, it is what the discussion is *around*.

Let me state something bluntly, coldly, and for the first time in public. I am the adult child of alcoholics, a victim of physical and psychological abuse. As a child, I was the victim of sexual molestation, so perhaps I have some expertise on this subject. Even so, "victim" is a term I still have a great deal of trouble applying to myself. The issue of consent is an important one—perhaps the most important.

I was twelve years old. It was 1962. There was no education about pedophiles, no concept of sexual molestation, no "don't get in cars with strangers," no "run and scream." Pedophilia was never discussed or thought about; it was a well-kept secret shame. I was walking happily to the local theater to take in a Saturday matinee: cartoons, a serial, maybe a horror movie or two. A man in his late twenties, driving a blue 1951 Ford hot rod, pulled up. He asked me if I could do him a favor and show him how to get to a place a short way out in the country, saying he had to meet a race car driver I had heard of and admired. I got in the car and took him to what, I later realized, was a terribly isolated and hidden part of the country outside town.

Thinking back on it, I realize I was well manipulated every step of the way into the car with visions of meeting a real, famous race-car driver. We went out into the clearing, and I took off my clothes to cross the creek. Sexually excited by pornography he just "happened" to have along, and my own natural curiosity, I was manipulated into the sexual act. He gave me an insulting amount of money, dropped me off at the theater and warned me to be silent—or I would be killed. Oh, yes, I was also manipulated into letting him take pictures of me.

In retrospect, I wonder why he didn't just kill me then. It was an isolated area. There were no witnesses. If I had been killed, nobody would have known, and my body might not have been found for a considerable time. That scares me.

And I did keep silent. I'm nearly forty-four years old now, and the molestation was buried in my memory until a few years ago, when it suddenly surfaced like a missile aimed at my life. In fact, this article is the first time that more than two or three people will know of, or even suspect the event. I never told my parents.

One of the reasons for this major emotional effect is the issue of consent. Because, you see, I did more or less "consent" to everything that happened—uninformed consent, surely, abetted by the handicap of a dysfunctional family who couldn't teach normality or right and wrong or, in fact, anything at all. While extremely well educated, I was an ignorant child, and am still ignorant in many commonsense ways.

Argue all you want. To a child, consent is a powerful thing. And, twenty-eight years later, I bear a heavy weight of guilt which grew from that uninformed consent. There is fear in knowing that photos were taken, areas of emotional affect that are as yet undefined and unexplored. That consent, however uninformed, manipulated, ignorant, was still consent.

What effect has this small, isolated moment had on my life? People who know me well know that I am a shattered, troubled man with a multitude of problems. Much of that can be attributed to my alcoholic family and to physical and psychological abuse. But it is difficult to separate those aspects from the molestation. In my mind, the alcoholism, the physical and psychological abuse, and the molestation all blend into a single issue; one of abuse and tragedy, one which carries, in all its aspects, a great deal of guilt.

I have a very real inability to express my emotions in normal ways; an obsession with sex, coupled with a sexual drive which is far above normal; and a definite streak of kinkiness. I have an obsessive need to be able to do things my own way, to control any situation I may find myself in. And an inability to keep relationships together, which cost me the greatest love of my life—twice. And always, there is the guilt and the fear, the terrible knowledge.

I studied martial arts, was involved in biker wars and vendettas, became fat and mean, so that I could intimidate people immediately, so that *no one* could ever make me a victim again. But there is still an issue of ignorant consent because, in my loves and lusts, I have made myself a victim of the women I have chosen. I have made myself a victim of failure, of poverty, of controversy, of homelessness, of starvation, of tragedy. I consistently, ignorantly, unconsciously have made the worst choices in every situation. In point of fact, I have become a victim in *every* way but the physical. Though I have attempted, in the last few years, to deal with these troubling issues, the things that happened to me as a child have effectively destroyed my life and endangered my survival; and they are still endangering my survival.

What, you may ask, does this have to do with a discussion of censorship and child pornography? Everything, because the victim is the issue. Let me say plainly and clearly that I am in favor of consensual pornography. I enjoy it, I support it, and, in fact, I have worked in the industry in years past. Consensual pornography is simply photographs or films which are intended for healthy stimulation and entertainment. No one is coerced or victimized or exploited, regardless of what you might have heard. Child pornography, on the other hand, is one of the single most horrendous crimes that can be committed. It is, as well, the visual evidence of a crime which is, in my opinion, more devastating than murder, and which should be treated as such.

Murder is the quick taking of a life. It's done, and it's over. Sexual molestation and abuse is slow, its effects often not showing for years. It burrows into the unconscious, rotting away the psyche. Its effects linger for a lifetime, the victims suffering the torture of having to live with the act and its ramifications of guilt and consent.

To add to the torture, if photos have been taken, the victim must then live with the terrible knowledge that somewhere out there, in someone's collection, or being passed around, looked at, masturbated over, and perhaps being used to manipulate other children, are pictures or films of their own victimization. There is a sense of your soul being held in filthy hands. One knows intellectually that a photo is only a piece of shiny paper. But emotionally there is a feeling of constant violation, of psychic rape. It tears at the psyche and tortures the emotions. It is not a one-time crime, but a violation which continues as long as the victim lives.

It's very, very difficult to express the emotions of a victim. It's not something which can really be put into words. When I talk about the things that happened to me, I shake and tremble, and my heart rate goes up considerably. There is, believe it or not, a certain sexual excitement which accompanies the memory, an excitement which deeply disturbs and repels me. There is an extreme lack of trust, so intense that when I was training to be a psychologist, going through my own analysis, I didn't even tell my therapist of the experience. Even now, although I am admitting to the experience, and "going public" with it, I would still not be able to talk to anyone about it with any efficacy. The crime, you see, continues.

My solution? Rather violent, I'm afraid. There is much talk of child molesters being sick and unable to control themselves, of compulsion and obsessions. Talk all you want—it makes no difference. I would happily take a sharp knife in hand, gut every one of them personally, and hang their bodies in public to rot. They have murdered lives and souls and minds. They deserve to die, horribly, preferably tortured beforehand, as their victims are tortured throughout a lifetime. These years, I am well known as the most gentle and loving of men; never anything but kind and loving to animals and small children. I have never struck or abused a woman or child, or even an animal, in my life. A gentle, loving man. But remember: I am also a victim.

BULLWHIPS, SEX SLAVES, AND *CATCHER IN THE RYE*

Stephen F. Rohde

Judging by recent events, the United States appears intent on commemorating the 200th anniversary of the Bill of Rights by stepping up the censorship of books, art, and music. As usual, the suppression of "obscenity" and "indecency" is trotted out as the excuse. From Mapplethorpe in Cincinnati, to 2 Live Crew in Florida, to over 240 attempts in 39 states to ban books from classrooms and libraries, there is a concerted effort to use criminal prosecutions and administrative proceedings to punish controversial ideas. Win or lose, the very initiation and perpetuation of these cases creates it own irremedial [sic] punishment in huge legal fees, lost energy, and —worst of all—self censorship.

Miller v. California

Since 1973, the U.S. Supreme Court has upheld obscenity laws which comply with a three-part test adopted in the case of *Miller* v. *California*, 413 U.S. 15. The prosecution must prove, beyond a reasonable doubt, that each of the following three tests has been met:

(a) whether "the average person, applying contemporary community standards" would find that the work, taken as whole, appeals to the prurient interest...;

(b) whether the work depicts or describes, in a patently offensive way, sexual conduct specifically defined by the applicable state law; and

(c) whether the work, taken as a whole, lacks serious literary, artistic, political, or scientific value.

In this country, only sex speech is subjected to censorship under these vague, elastic, and oppressive standards. When it comes to other subject matter, having nothing to do with sex, the First Amendment would not tolerate the punishment of speech because it did not conform to "contemporary community standards" (whatever that means), or was "patently offensive" to any twelve jurors, or failed to achieve a level of "serious literary, artistic, political or scientific value." If the utterances of our elected officials, talk-show guests and hosts, romance novelists, stand-up comedians or other assorted "opinion makers" were judged by such standards, most of them would be in jail.

Anthony Comstock and Rev. Donald Wildmon

But the fact that obscenity laws purport to censor only sex speech should not suggest that they were not intended or enforced to suppress a far wider range of controversial ideas and purposely to accustom the public to governmental control of what we can see, read and do.

The father of modern American obscenity laws was Anthony Comstock. Born in 1844, he served two yeas in the Union Army during the Civil War and kept a diary brimming with confessions of his struggle with temptation. In 1872 he founded the New York Society for the Suppression of Vice and led his first raid on a bookstore. From the outset, Comstock pursued twin goals: the eradication of obscenity and the banning of "abortifacients and contraceptives." Here we see the ominous linkage between restricting freedom of speech and restricting freedom of choice which persists to this day.

According to Comstock's reports, between 1872 and 1874, his Society and accommodating police officers, seized 130,000 pounds of books and 60,300 "articles of rubber made for immoral purposes, and used by both sexes."

Comstock widened his horizons and lobbied Congress to pass a new law prohibiting the use of the mails or advertising to sell obscene literature and items "for the prevention of conception." The law would serve as a model for similar "Comstock" statutes in twenty-two states.

As soon as President Ulysses S. Grant signed the bill, he appointed Comstock a special postal inspector, an official position he held until his death in 1915. In his first fifteen years, Comstock made 1,200 arrests, seizing a wide variety of books and artworks. In 1906 he raided the Art Students League in New York because the school used nude models. Comstock led the fight to prosecute Margaret Sanger, a founder of the birth-control movement.

Today Comstock's work is carried on by such groups as the American Family Association (AFA), with 535 chapters in all fifty states, headed by Rev. Donald Wildmon of Tupelo, Mississippi. Wildmon's brother Allen, a spokesman for the AFA, is not shy about the AFA's real agenda. "Whose set of values is going to dominate in society?" he asks. The attack on the National Endowment for the Arts, Wildmon explains, "is just one spoke in the wheel as far as the overall picture—you've got rock music, you've got abortion. Somebody's values are going to dominate. Is it going to be a humanistic set of values, or a 'biblical' set of values?"

Mapplethorpe in "Censornati"

For the first time in American history, on April 7, 1990, an art museum was indicted for obscenity. The Cincinnati Contemporary Arts Center had just opened an exhibit entitled

"The Perfect Moment": 175 photographs by the late Robert Mapplethorpe, a renowned photographer whose works ranged from still lifes of calla lilies and orchids to sexually explicit homoerotic portraits. In 1984 the NEA had awarded Mapplethorpe a $15,000 fellowship and in 1988 had paid $30,000 to help defray the cost of mounting "The Perfect Moment" at the Institute of Contemporary Art at the University of Pennsylvania.

Cincinnati has long been a hotbed (cold bed?) of censorship. In 1957, Cincinnati businessman Charles Keating (yes, that Charles Keating) founded Citizens for Decent Literature (later renamed Citizens for Decency Through Law). Before moving to Phoenix (to build his ill-fated S&L fortune), Keating passed the anti-smut mantle to Rev. Jerry Kirk, who founded the National Coalition against Pornography and Citizens for Community Values, which actively pushed for the indictment of the Arts Center and its director, Dennis Barrie.

The trial began here on September 24, 1990. At stake were seven of the 175 Mapplethorpe photographs. All were part of a special portion of the exhibit from which children had been excluded. Five portrayed graphic depictions of homoeroticism, including a self-portrait of Mapplethorpe with a bullwhip in his ass and another showing one man pissing into another man's mouth. The other two were photographs of young children in various states of nudity with their genitals partially exposed.

Almost without exception, observers believed that Barrie and the Arts Center would be convicted, and that the case would then depend on the dispassionate review of an appellate court. The jury pool didn't give the defendants much hope. Most said they didn't read newspapers. Most could count their visits to any kind of museum on a single hand. And most lived in the conservative suburbs surrounding Cincinnati. When one prospective juror admitted she had worked for Rev. Kirk, had attended a convention of the National Coalition Against Pornography, had subscribed to the CCV newsletter, and, after seeing photocopies of the Mapplethorpe photographs in March, had formed the opinion that they should never be displayed any time, anywhere, for any reason, the trial judge *still* refused to exclude her "for cause" because she said she could be a fair and impartial juror. (The defense used one of its six peremptory challenges to get her off the jury.) The prosecution's entire case in chief was simply to present the photographs to the jury. No expert testimony. As prosecutor Frank Prouty put it in his opening statement: "You have the chance to decide on your own—where do you draw the line? Are these the kinds of pictures that should be permitted in the museum?"

By contrast, the defense put on an elaborate series of expert witnesses testifying to the artistic merit of the Mapplethorpe exhibit. Defense lawyers Lou Sirkin and Marc Mezibov knew that to win the case they had to prevail on the third prong of the Miller test: to convince the jury that no matter how "prurient" or "patently offensive," the Mapplethorpe photographs had "serious artistic value." To do so, they called Janet Kardon, the curator of the show in Philadelphia; Jacqueline Baas, director of the University of California Art Museum (Berkeley); John Walsh, director of the J. Paul Getty Museum (Malibu); and Robert Sobieszek, former curator at the George Eastman House (Rochester, New York). Each in his or her own way explained why these sometimes-shocking photographs were works of art.

The defense concluded its case by reading from sworn depositions given by the mothers of Jesse and Rosie, the two children photographed by Mapplethorpe. Both were friends of the photographer and had willing consented and encouraged the photographs and were present when they were taken.

The first public sign that the prosecution didn't think a guilty verdict was in the bag came when Prouty called his one-and-only expert witness in rebuttal. The defense experts had apparently made such an impact on Prouty that he decided they could not go unchallenged. For this task he chose Dr. Judith Reisman. A former research director for Wildmon's AFA, she had written an article for the *Washington Times* (the Moonie-owned daily, not to be confused with the *Washington Post*) on Mapplethorpe, titled "Promoting Child Abuse as Art." One other qualification was revealed; for some years, she had served as a songwriter for Captain Kangaroo.

Over a defense objection that Reisman would serve "no purpose other than to pollute the jury with unqualified testimony," the trial judge allowed her to take the stand.

Generally, Dr. Reisman testified that the photographs were not art. Ironically, of the bullwhip photo, she conceded, "This would be one of the only photos that might offer emotion, but the face is blank. It says, 'I am here.'" By admitting that it said anything—that it communicated any message—Dr. Reisman may have netted the defense a slight advantage.

Utilizing the "inoculation theory" (the notion that an advocate advances his theory by acknowledging a small dose of the other side's argument, thereby inoculating the jury from its powerful impact if ignored), Sirkin, in his closing remarks, referred to some of the photographs as ugly and possibly offensive, but argued that art did not always have to be pretty. Sobieszek had described the photographs as "a search for understanding, like Van Gogh painting himself with his ear cut off." Mezibov urged the jurors "to show the country that this is a community of tolerant and sensitive people."

Prouty appealed to a different sense of civic pride. He urged them to let the world know that Cincinnati was different from other cities. He ridiculed expert Jacqueline Baas ("she's from California") and he argued that the art world thinks it's above the law. ("They're saying they're better than us [sic].")

On October 5, 1990, after only three hours of deliberation, the eight-person jury found Barrie and the Arts Center not guilty on all charges. "The prosecution basically decided to show us the pictures so that we'd say they weren't art when everybody else was telling us they were," said juror Anthony Eckstein. "The defendants were innocent until proven guilty, and they didn't prove them guilty."

Once the glow of the victory faded, it was apparent that the First Amendment had escaped only by the figurative skin of its teeth. Had the prosecution called any number of the scores of self-appointed experts on child pornography, obscenity, and the resulting "disintegration of the American family," the jury might have had something on which to hang a guilty verdict.

Even the acquittal did not come without its costs. Barrie and the Arts Center incurred $325,000 in expenses for expert witnesses, transcripts, court costs, and legal fees (even though a considerable amount of legal work was contributed pro bono). Add to that the hundreds of hours spent by Barrie and his staff—precious time stolen from the work of administering the Arts Center. And finally the intimidating risk to others that they could face a year in prison and $10,000 in fines for creating or exhibiting art.

2 Live Crew in Broward County

Meanwhile, across the country in Fort Lauderdale, Florida, the First Amendment could claim only a split decision. In separate prosecutions, on October 2, 1990, Charles Freeman, a record-store owner, was convicted of selling the notorious 2 Live Crew album, *As Nasty as They Wanna Be*, while on October 20, 1990, the group itself was acquitted for performing several songs from the album at a nightclub.

It is difficult to tell whether Mapplethorpe's homoerotic photographs or 2 Live Crew's sexist rap lyrics are more outside the mainstream of America's dominant culture. It is not difficult to see that both of these obscenity prosecutions attack minority life-styles which deliberately challenge middle-class values. Of course the protection of minority viewpoints from majority control is exactly what the First Amendment is all about. The majority doesn't need special constitutional protection for the expression of its ideas, it has the votes. It is minority viewpoints, from blacks, gays, radicals, extremists, atheists, and other dissidents that need protection. But when the law, as in the case of obscenity, allows the prosecution to use the very unorthodox nature of expression itself to prove criminal responsibility, it is remarkable for any juror to rise above his or her own personal objections to such controversial ideas and still vote for acquittal.

2 Live Crew's misogynist lyrics are a perfect example. They portray a world of sex slaves and turgid males, as in, "He'll tear the cunt open 'cause it's satisfaction" and "Grabbed one by the hair, threw her on the floor, opened up her thighs and guess what I saw." The songs on *As Nasty as They Wanna Be* refer endlessly to male and female genitalia, human sexual excretion, oral-anal contact, fellatio, group sex, erections, masturbation, cunnilingus, and sexual intercourse.

To blunt the threats of an obscenity indictment, 2 Live Crew's attorney, Bruce Rogow, a law professor at Nova University in Fort Lauderdale, seized the offensive and filed a declaratory relief action in Federal District Court. The strategy was to preempt the prosecution by securing a Federal Court determination that *As Nasty As They Wanna Be* was not obscene under *Miller*.

The plan backfired.

On June 6, 1990, U.S. District Judge Jose A. Gonzalez, Jr., declared the album obscene. Frankly, any legal opinion that begins by misquoting Oliver Wendell Holmes can't be all good. He began by invoking Holmes's decision in a 1919 U.S. Supreme Court case to show that "the First Amendment is not absolute and that it does not permit one to yell 'Fire' in a crowded theatre [sic]." What Justice Holmes actually wrote was "The most stringent protection of free speech would not protect a man in *falsely* shouting 'fire' in a crowded theater *and causing a panic.*" (*Emphasis added.*)

It was not the mere utterance that criminalized the speech, it was the added facts that (a) the speech was false, and (b) the speech actually caused panic. That one often hears Justice Holmes misquoted at cocktail parties is lamentable; that a federal judge should ground his legal opinion on such a mistake is irresponsible.

Not that that was Judge Gonzalez's only mistake. When it came time for him to decide whether *Nasty,* taken as a whole, lacked "serious literary, artistic, political, or scientific value," Judge Gonzalez exposed an extraordinary case of cultural myopia and artistic narrow-mindedness.

2 Live Crew had offered the testimony of Professor Carlton Long, who was qualified as an expert on black American culture. Professor Long testified to the political message in the album, including its commentary on Abraham Lincoln in the song "Dirty Nursery Rhymes" and the repeated use of the device of "boasting" to stress one's manhood. Without explanation, Judge Gonzalez concluded that the album lacked any "serious political value."

Professor Long also found genuine sociological value in the devices of "call and response" ("Tastes Great—Less Filling," parodying the beer commercial), "doing the dozens" (a word game which Judge Gonzalez himself recognized as "a series of insults escalating in their satirical content") and "boasting" (a device where persons "overstate their virtues such as sexual prowess"). In a remarkable act of logical legerdemain, Judge Gonzalez concluded that since these devices were "part of the universal human condition," not exclusive to the culture of black Americans, they could be ignored in judging the value of the album.

That Judge Gonzalez had already decided to find the album obscene, and was merely going through the motions of appearing to give due consideration to the evidence presented by 2 Live Crew, is obvious from his superficial dismissal of the album's artistic value. Acknowledging that the group stressed the album's value as "comedy and satire," Judge Gonzalez did not so much as disagree with that characterization as he revealed that he really didn't get the joke. Betraying total ignorance of the role of satire, he simply could not imagine reasonable people finding anything funny about the album's treatment of violence, perversion, sex, and genitals. Of course, the very fact that he had to address this issue served as the best evidence of the album's artistic value. Having elsewhere conceded that "this court's role is not to serve as a censor or an art and music critic," Judge Gonzalez proceeded to act just like one.

Fortunately, Judge Gonzalez's decision came in a civil case, not in a criminal case. It was not binding on any Florida criminal court, but it had the demoralizing impact of letting the authorities claim that 2 Live Crew and other purveyors of the *Nasty* album were now "on notice" that they were circulating "obscene" material.

Two days after Judge Gonzalez's ruling, Charles Freeman was arrested at his record store for selling a copy of the album to an adult undercover cop in Fort Lauderdale. And two days after that, three of 2 Live Crew, including leader Luther Campbell, were arrested for performing their songs at an adults-only concert.

Freeman, who sold about 1,000 copies of the album netting him about $3,000, was convicted, while Campbell and the others, who have sold more that two million copies, earning them approximately six million dollars, were acquitted. It's hard to tell what made the difference. Constitutional lawyer Rogow handled the defense in both trials. Freeman was tried first, before an all-white jury. Campbell's jury included one black. In Freeman's case, the Nasty album itself was on trial. In Campbell's case, the prosecution was burdened with a barely audible tape of the live performance. Regrettably, the first trial may have served as a dress rehearsal for the second, where Rogow, the experts, and even the jurors themselves appeared not to take the rap music so seriously and often punctuated the testimony with irrepressible laughter. This obviously helped Campbell, who maintained all along that his music was supposed to make people happy.

Campbell also had help from Henry L. Gates, professor of literature at Duke University, who called 2 Live Crew's music "astonishing and refreshing." Lacing his testimony with allusions to Shakespeare, Chaucer, Eddie Murphy, Ella Fitzgerald, and James Brown, Gates said that the group had taken stereotypes of black men—as oversexed, hypersexed, in an unhealthy way—and blown them up. "You have to bust out laughing."

The jury bought it. "We agreed with what he [Gates] said about this being like Archie Bunker making fun of racism," according to jury foreman David Garsow, a twenty-four year-old office clerk, who sings at the Key Biscayne Presbyterian Church. Helena Bailie, a retired sociology professor from New York, said she admired what fellow juror, Beverly Resnick, sixty-five, had said during the deliberations: "You take away one freedom, and pretty soon they're all gone."

On December 12, 1990, Freeman was fined $1,000 by Broward County Judge Paul L. Backman. In a transparent effort to sugarcoat his ruling, Judge Backman ordered Freeman to pay the fine to the Walker Elementary School, which specializes in the performing arts and had recently had much of its musical equipment stolen. Freeman, who could have been sent to jail for one year, vowed to appeal "all the way to the U.S. Supreme Court."

But Freeman may receive a chilly reception in the High

Court. Fortified by the confirmation of David Souter, the conservative majority, led by Chief Justice William Rehnquist, could uphold Freeman's conviction by deferring to the "community standards" of Broward County, regardless of the consensus of constitutional scholars that the question of "artistic value" under the third prong of the "Miller test" should be judged by an objective national standard, free from parochial idiosyncrasies.

Of course, the Supreme Court may become 2 Live Crew aficionados before they dispose of all the 2 Live Crew cases working their way through the courts. Several prosecutions have been initiated in Texas and North Carolina; in Calcasieu Parish, Louisiana, Judge E. Woody Thompson enjoined a record store from selling the *As Nasty as They Wanna Be* album, after listening to one song, "Me So Horny."

"The Censorship Movement in America is Flourishing"

With those words, Arthur Kropp, president of People for the American Way, released the organization's eighth annual survey on book censorship in America's schools. The 244 attempts in the 1989–90 school year represented a forty percent increase above the 172 attempts the prior year. But more chilling than these statistics is a sample of titles that came under attack last year:

The Hobbit, by J. R. R. Tolkien, which was accused of promoting Satanism; *The Red Pony* and *Of Mice and Men,* by John Steinbeck, for offensive language, *Where the Sidewalk Ends* and *A Light in the Attic,* by Shel Silverstein, for promoting disruptive behavior and for sexual innuendos and demonic overtones; *Catcher in the Rye,* by J. D. Salinger, for offensive language; *Cujo,* by Stephen King, for profanity and sexually explicit content; *The Color Purple,* by Alice Walker, for undermining family values; *Little Red Riding Hood,* for its depiction of a grandmother drinking wine; *Blubber,* by Judy Blume, for offensive language; *Night,* by Elie Wiesel, because it is "depressing" and inappropriate because the past should be forgotten; and *Capital,* by Karl Marx, for being politically subversive.

Meanwhile, through parliamentary sleight of hand during

the reauthorization of the National Endowment for the Arts, Jesse Helms replaced a vague and unconstitutional ban on the funding of "obscenity" with a limitless and unconstitutional ban on "indecency." Reelected for six more years, Helms set the agenda for the 1990s: "I say to all the arts community and to all homosexuals: You ain't seen nothing yet!"

THE ARGUMENTS AGAINST PORNOGRAPHY

Jim Bramlett

Harry Truman once remarked about the America of his youth: "In those days, right was right and wrong was wrong, and you didn't have to talk about it."

Today, some people seem confused about what is right and wrong, forcing us to talk about it, and write articles. Values, however, are only one of the many arguments against pornography. Law, science and logic are our main weapons.

Porn's Principal Proponents

The loudest pro-porn voices—such as the peddlers (including organized crime) and their lawyers—have vested financial interests, so their arguments are tainted and can be discounted accordingly. Pornography is an $8–10 billion industry. Fortunes are at stake. It is not surprising that pornography is organized crime's third-largest money-maker, mostly tax-free, behind only gambling and prostitution.

There is only one other major porn advocate: predictably, the American Civil Liberties Union (ACLU), the group founded by avowed radical socialist Robert [sic] Baldwin, who made no secret of his intent to destroy, not uphold, the American system. His professed strategy was to exploit America's freedoms for his perverted purpose. Baldwin said, "Civil liberties, like democracy, are only useful as tools for social change. Political democracy as such a tool is obviously bankrupt." By continuing to exploit the "freedom issue," the ACLU has been faithful to its founder's methodology.

Whom shall we believe? Shall we believe the porn profiteers, organized crime, and the ACLU? Or shall we believe the often poorly paid social workers, or rape victims, or molestation sufferers, or hurting parents who have seen the ugly ravages of this exploitation; or the clergy who have often buried its victims? Take your choice. Here are the facts.

The Legal Argument

The hollow cry of the porn proponents is "freedom of speech" (from the First Amendment, now called "freedom of expression" by some). However, no rational person believes in totally free expression, without limits. We can stop someone from crying "Fire" in a crowded theater. We can stop someone from revealing national secrets to a foreign enemy. There are laws against libel, slander, and false advertising. We can prevent a couple from copulating openly in a public shopping mall. We can also draw the line elsewhere if personal harm may be caused or public sensitivities outraged. Your freedom stops where my space begins.

Thankfully, we live in a nation where our freedom of speech is constitutionally guaranteed by the First Amendment, a feature that has helped preserve our great republic. But all freedoms have limits, plus constitutional provisions must be interpreted, a job the Constitution assigns to the Supreme Court. And the Supreme

Court has ruled that free speech has its limits. For example, in 1973 the Court ruled in *Miller* v. *California* that obscenity is clearly not protected by the First Amendment. There are more than two dozen other landmark Supreme Court rulings against obscenity. Another 1973 ruling explained:

"The sum of experience affords an ample basis...to conclude that a sensitive, key relationship of human existence, central to family life, community welfare, and the development of the human personality, can be debased and distorted by crass commercial exploitation of sex."

Strangely, some still cry "censorship." But when there are laws that prohibit obscenity, and when judges and juries uphold these laws, it is not censorship, but democracy in action. Also oddly, those protesting censorship about "freedom of speech," the second clause of the First Amendment, in practice just as strongly oppose and try to censor the "free exercise" (first) clause of the same amendment, exposing their contradiction and real agenda.

But simply stated: There is no constitutional freedom of speech argument for hard-core pornography. Case closed.

The Victimization Argument

Aside from its lack of constitutional protection, let's consider pornography on its own demerits. Mindlessly, proponents claim it is "victimless." Nothing could be further from the truth. There is overwhelming, voluminous, and incontrovertible proof of pornography's personal and social harm. It exploits the models and actors, such as runaway children and prostitutes. As to its users, numerous scientific studies have proven beyond doubt that pornography is addictive and progressive, and that there is a strong cause-and-effect relationship between pornography and loss of respect for women, rape, child molestation, sexual deviance, and violent crime. The recent "Final Report of the Attorney General's Commission on Pornography" makes a totally compelling case. Naturally, the commission's report was assailed and distorted by the porn industry—and the ACLU. Also, interestingly, the report was actually "censored" by the media by giving this epic social commentary only scant coverage. For example, one observer said that at all three commission sessions, almost the only people he saw were from *Playboy*, *Penthouse*, and *Forum* magazines—and the ACLU. The TV networks and major print media made only token appearances. Maybe it is not surprising, since they are all guilty of commercial sexploitation.

Fortunately, the media do not have to convince most citizens of pornography's harm, such as the 1,400 child-molestation victims in Louisville, where openly displayed pornography was found in each and every home; or the 48,000 sex-crime victims in Michigan, where forty-one percent of the perpetrators, according to the Michigan State Police, were involved with pornography; or the family of pretty Linda Daniels, whose abductors filmed her repeated rape throughout the night in order to make a pornographic film, then they brutally murdered her. Residents in one Cincinnati neighborhood are probably also convinced after major crimes such as rape, robbery, and assault dropped eighty-three percent when adult bookstores and X-rated theaters were closed.

The Values Argument

Many like to repeat the old clichés, "You cannot legislate morality," or "You cannot impose your values on others." Nonsense. That is what the entire legal system is all about: the codification of a culture's values and mores. It is just a question of whose values we codify. Porn peddlers would like to legislate their own definition of morality and impose their own values on the rest of us.

Historically, like it or not, America's values have been rooted in Judeo-Christian principles covering murder, theft, sexual morality, and other "value subjects" as well as treasured concepts such as private property and free enterprise. Morality was first codified about thirty-five hundred years ago when Moses was given the Ten Commandments on Mount Sinai; about two thousand years ago, Christ affirmed them and explained their deeper intent. According to famous British historian Arnold Toynbee, these principles and the Jewish and Christian Scriptures were the chrysalis from which the entire Western civilization emerged. Today, thanks to our foundations, America stands alone as a consistent beacon of democracy and progress. Our greatest threat is unbridled freedom without responsibility and degeneration from within.

Certainly, one may reject these truths, but don't be misled. This is not an issue just for religious "extremists" as some would like us to believe. The idea that pornography is harmful has been "mainstreamed," according to Pornography Commissioner Bruce Ritter.

On July 25, 1986, religious leaders representing 150 million Americans met and endorsed the commission's report and priorities. Included were Catholic, Protestant, and Jewish representatives in one of the most profound displays of religious unity in human history. If you did not hear about it, it is because the momentous event did not get thirty seconds of coverage on the three major television networks, or one paragraph from three major news magazines, a testimony of media's own values.

Rabbi Marc Tanenbaum of the American Jewish Committee, said:

> No one who walks through the streets of [his city] can help but feel that there is a social pathology, a plague and a pestilence which daily dishonors the dignity of life of our people. There is a moral ecology in the world...that is assaulted by the prevalence of drugs, crack, prostitution, the decline of the family and crime. *Pornography both contributes to that and is a symbol of moral decadence of our nation.* (Emphasis supplied.)

Rabbi Tanenbaum articulates what most of us feel as we observe that has happened in our nation during the past few decades. Our apathy let it go too far. But many people are now aroused, and they're not going to take any anymore.

Conclusion

There is no rational argument for the free expression of pornography. It is not a constitutional freedom. It has proven to have a high victim rate. It is contrary to the predominant values and mores of our culture. It benefits only one group: it makes money for its peddlers, especially for organized crime. It is an unconscionable, indefensible blight upon society.

ABOVE THE LAW:
THE JUSTICE DEPARTMENT'S WAR AGAINST THE FIRST AMENDMENT

The American Civil Liberties Union Art Censorship Project
Marjorie Heins, Director

Imagine a small group of government lawyers taking it upon themselves to decide what Americans should be allowed to read, listen to, and watch. Imagine that they are aware that their brand of censorship violates the First Amendment, but that they do not care. Imagine that, in the name of their own personal sense of morality, they are willing to break the law in a crusade to banish from the marketplace publications, recordings, art, and films that are legal but have more sexual content than these lawyers deem appropriate.

In reality, no feat of imagination is necessary. The small group of lawyers behind this constitutionally renegade operation are members of the National Obscenity Enforcement Unit in the U.S. Department of Justice. If they are permitted to continue their extralegal campaign to rid the country of sexually oriented material, it is hard not to imagine the broad range of creative works that might be targeted for banishment next.

Ostensibly, the Justice Department unit (recently renamed "Child Exploitation and Obscenity Section") was created to bring criminal prosecutions against distributors of obscene materials—materials that the Supreme Court has held to be without constitutional protection. To pursue its own agenda, however, the unit has devised a strategy of bankrupting distributors of non-obscene sexually oriented materials by making them go to the considerable expense of defending simultaneous multiple prosecutions in far-flung jurisdictions. The unit does not seem to care whether it can win convictions in the cases it brings; it often knows the cases are not winnable. Instead, it seeks to drain its targets financially, to make the defense of constitutional rights in many places at once so costly that distributors will abandon their businesses rather than suffer the continuing economic loss.

Not surprisingly, the unit has succeeded in driving a number of companies out of business by forcing them to accept plea bargains that rob them of their future ability to distribute constitutionally protected expressive materials. As part of their pleas, the distributors typically must agree to stop selling *any* "sexually oriented" literature or films. And the chilling effects of these prosecutions are reverberating throughout the country, narrowing the variety of artistic and social expression available to the public.

The number of tax dollars and the amount of law-enforcement resources being expended on this censorship effort should be matters of serious concern not only to those who care about freedom of expression, but to those who are concerned with waste of government resources. The expenditure of small amounts of money on federal grants to a few artists whose work offends the sensibilities of some viewers—an issue that has created so much heat in Washington and throughout the country—pales in comparison to the Justice Department's misguided expenditures to stamp out sexually explicit art.

The tactics used by the Justice Department to suppress sexually oriented work violate constitutional free expression guarantees and could not withstand judicial scrutiny. As the Supreme Court has held repeatedly, the Constitution requires that efforts directed at obscenity "conform to procedures that will ensure against the curtailment of constitutionally protected expression, which is often separated from obscenity only by a dim and uncertain line." The difficulty that both courts and juries have had in separating obscene material that is illegal from sexually oriented material that is not, has been exploited by the unit to chill the speech of many legitimate distributors, publishers and artists.

Success breeds imitation, and a successful strategy of bankrupting disfavored publishers, distributors, and moviemakers will inspire new targets and new issues. Moreover, it will encourage more people to accuse disfavored speech, whether or not sexual in nature, of being "obscene." In Washington, D.C., earlier this year, on behalf of the Roman Catholic Archdiocese, Monsignor William E. Lori asked the public transportation authority to remove a particular political advertisement that he termed "anti-Catholic" and therefore obscene. Metro officials refused, but the use of the obscenity label was part of a stratagem to remove the material from the First Amendment's orbit. If the battle cry of obscenity can be used as an excuse in one instance to censor protected speech, it can become the focal point of subsequent assaults on other forms of free expression.

The Justice Department's flouting of constitutionally required procedural safeguards in obscenity prosecutions amounts to nothing less than the use of governmental power to force the financial ruin of distributors of expressive works that a small group within the government finds offensive. As we have learned from our country's history, the first victims of repression are never the last. If the Obscenity Unit is permitted to continue its repressive campaign, others who speak out and are unpopular with those holding the reins of government will be placed in danger.

This report includes a history of the Justice Department unit, which started as an offshoot of the controversial Meese Commission. It provides examples of the unit's unconstitutional activities and discusses the broad First Amendment implications of its attacks. The report ends with the demand that the Justice Department's obscenity unit be disbanded and that, in the interim, Congress conduct oversight hearings on its activities.

Prologue: The Meese Commission

In 1967, President Lyndon Johnson appointed a commission, including physicians, sociologists, and researchers, to study the role of sexually explicit material in American society. After conducting a thorough review of existing literature and hearing from experts, the commission issued a report in 1970. Its conclusion: no convincing evidence tied pornography to antisocial behavior, and no new laws were needed to restrict it. Indeed, the commission recommended that there be more—not less—public discussion and examination of human sexuality.

In 1985, under the growing influence of the fundamentalist anti-pornography movement, the Reagan Administration's Attorney General, Edwin Meese, created a new commission to study the effects of pornography on American life. The Meese Commission had a far less objective agenda. Its chairman, Henry Hudson, was a Virginia prosecutor who had gone on a one-man crusade to eliminate all adult bookstores and theaters in Arlington County. Another commissioner, Park Dietz, had said that network television programs like *Miami Vice* and *Hunter*, although not legally obscene, were "the most harmful form of pornography." And the commission's executive director, Alan Sears, went on to become one of the legal counsel for Charles Keating's right-wing Citizens for Decency Through Law.

Despite Meese's protestations that the eleven members of the commission did not "come to the task with their minds made up," six members had declared their opposition to pornography, and two others supported efforts that would have limited distribution of sexually explicit materials. The remaining three members had no declared positions on the issue.

The Meese Commission skewed research results in order to

lend credence to its preordained conclusions. To determine whether pornography was becoming increasingly violent, for example, the commission examined the April 1986 issues of top-selling sexually explicit magazines, including *Playboy, Penthouse, Hustler, High Society,* and *Genesis.* The commission's final report never mentions the result of that study: that only 0.6 percent of the imagery was of "force, violence, or weapons." Instead, it suppressed the results of its own research and used data from a 1983 study by the Canadian National Commission, which had found that ten percent of the imagery in adult magazines involved "force." Moreover, the Meese Commission suppressed a report that it had commissioned by Surgeon General Everett Koop that questioned the validity of the commission's "scientific findings."

Witnesses who opposed government attempts to censor sexually explicit material were badgered, vigorously cross-examined, and grilled about a variety of tangential issues designed to cast doubt on their credibility. In cases where their testimony did not fit the commission's suppositions, it was simply ignored. The commission sought no testimony from writers' groups or the creative community, and denied many prominent organizations an opportunity to speak.

Given the commission's highly subjective approach, it was not surprising that its report, delivered in early 1986, discovered a "link" between violence and pornography that had previously confounded social scientists. Based on lurid, anecdotal testimony and selected research results, the commission concluded that exposure to pornography caused viewers to commit acts of sexual violence—a conclusion that was subsequently rejected by the researchers upon whose work the report was supposedly based. The commission's work was such an embarrassment that two members, Judith Becker and Ellen Levine, dissented, noting that "the commission's methods themselves have hindered the adequate pursuit of information"; that the commission lacked the "time and money to complete a thorough study"; that there was a "paucity" of expert opinion and an "absence of significant debate."

Despite the many deficiencies of the commission's approach,

its ninety-two recommendations led to extensive changes in federal legislation, such as forfeiture provisions that allow prosecutors to seize assets of stores renting both mainstream and adult videotapes, and rigorous record-keeping and labeling requirements for *any* sexually explicit photograph or film. One of the most damaging to free speech was Recommendation #12, which read: "The attorney general should appoint a high-ranking official from the Department of Justice to oversee the creation and operation of an obscenity task force." Under the guidance of the religious right, the National Obscenity Enforcement Unit has since grown to a thirteen-lawyer prosecutorial hit squad, spending millions of taxpayers' dollars to punish and suppress free expression about sexuality.

The National Obscenity Enforcement Unit

Like the Meese Commission, the National Obscenity Enforcement Unit was from the start firmly biased against "sexually oriented" literature and films. Following the Meese Commission's report, the unit embarked on a crusade to remove sexually oriented material of all kinds from the marketplace, regardless of whether or not it was ever likely to be ruled legally obscene. Leading the crusade were overzealous United States Attorneys who sought to decide for the rest of the country what was acceptable reading and viewing material.

Beginning in 1987, on the recommendation of the Meese Commission, the National Obscenity Enforcement Unit set up shop in the Justice Department. H. Robert Showers, a former U.S. Attorney in North Carolina, served as director, but he and Brent Ward, the U.S. Attorney for Utah, worked together establishing policy. According to Robert Marinaro, the agent in charge of FBI investigations of obscenity, "It was unclear at times who is in charge of NOEU, Brent Ward or Rob Showers." Their shared goal was to drive distributors of sexually oriented material out of business in any way possible. They wanted to "stop the flow of both soft-core and hard-core" pornography, Marinaro testified in a sworn deposition taken during a civil suit against the Justice Department.

The heart of the unit's strategy, as outlined in a 1985 letter from Ward to Meese, was for "multiple prosecutions (either simultaneous or successive) at all levels of government in many locations... This strategy would test the limits of pornographers' endurance." The unit went about identifying jurisdictions in which the community standards were favorable to obscenity prosecutions, and then it prosecuted the same distributors in several of these jurisdictions simultaneously.

Yet, at the same time, the unit had to be careful not to indict a firm in the district where it was actually located, in order to avoid consolidation motions by the defense, which would "destroy the multiple-prosecution impact." The unit therefore deliberately excluded many districts as possible venues for prosecution in order to avoid consolidation motions.

Any firms that managed to survive the multiple prosecution assault would be prosecuted in their own district for "a continuing criminal enterprise under the RICO [Racketeering Influenced and Corrupt Organizations] statute," a piece of legislation originally created to deal with organized crime.

The unit also brought obscenity charges against different parts or subsidiaries of the same business, thereby charging two or more individuals in the same company with separate offenses. FBI agent Marinaro confirmed that "the strategy basically was to maximize the cost of defense to the pornographer by charging [in] different districts, by charging employees of the company separately." Ward and Showers believed that the distributors would find it "very difficult...to be defending themselves since there were a limited number...of First Amendment lawyers [capable] of defending these organizations." According to Marinaro, the unit was "hoping to tie them [the lawyers] up as much as possible."

This strategy, however, directly contradicted the Justice Department's own rules, as set forth in the U.S. Attorney's Manual, which specifically discouraged simultaneous multiple prosecutions, because of the "unfairness associated with [them]." Undeterred, Ward and Showers drafted a new section for the policy manual that actually encouraged the use of multiple prosecutions, but *only* for obscenity cases. The old policy had allowed multiple prosecutions only in narrow circumstances where there was "no question" as to the legal obscenity of the material. The revised policy removes this language, encourages multiple prosecutions, and refers only to "the nature of the material." The new policy centralizes control of multi-district prosecutions in the Obscenity Unit.

Ward and Showers ignored warnings from local prosecutors and national staff that the multiple prosecution strategy was unconstitutional and would embarrass the government. Martin Littlefield, Assistant U.S. Attorney for the Western District of New York, wrote to Showers and Ward in July 1988, telling them that the multiple prosecutions could produce "a very distasteful, if not embarrassing, situation to the United States Government," because the First Amendment "essentially prohibits Governmental activity which would put these companies out of business."

Littlefield had been trying to prosecute Tao Productions, a small distributor of soft-core materials—such as films of female mud wrestlers—and he was concerned that simultaneous prosecutions by the unit in Utah and Arkansas would cause the company to go out of business before a jury could rule on the obscenity issue. Littlefield reminded Ward, Showers, and Utah Assistant U.S. Attorney Richard Lambert that multi-district prosecutions to put Tao out of business would violate constitutional principles. The unit ultimately dropped the prosecutions against Tao in Arkansas and Utah, but continued with the multiple-prosecution strategy elsewhere.

Meanwhile, the unit was pumping tax dollars and governmental resources into the support of dubious, extremist, private "anti-pornography" groups. The unit has co-sponsored conferences during the last three years on fighting pornography with an organization called Bay Area Citizens Against Pornography or BACAP, whose fundamentalist views and materials attempt to link pornography with "Satanism."

Working with the U.S. Post Office (which maintains the power to regulate interstate transportation of obscene materials through the mails), in July 1988 the Obscenity Unit launched Project PostPorn," a multiple-prosecution campaign against national mail-order distributors of sexually oriented material. PostPorn's stated goals, according to an NOEU internal memorandum, were:

"To have a significant impact on the mail-order distribution market."

"To put major mail-order obscenity distributors out of business."

The creation of Project PostPorn led one of the unit's attorneys, Paul McCommon, to write an extensive and detailed memo to Showers in September 1988, raising many of the same constitutional concerns about the multiple-prosecution strategy that the U.S. Attorney Littlefield had raised earlier in the year:

"Over the past year, I have become increasingly concerned about 'Project PostPorn,' and the practice of simultaneous multiple prosecutions," McCommon wrote. "On several occasions I have advised you of my concerns, but I don't feel you have taken my warnings seriously." McCommon further advised Showers that multiple prosecutions orchestrated from Washington could easily be viewed by judges as "improper forum shopping," warned of the First Amendment problems, and reiterated that the unit could be engaging in ethical violations. Showers ordered McCommon to shred all copies of the memo, a decision that led to Showers's suspension and ultimate removal from office.

To ensure that few, if any, firms survived the multiple-prosecution strategy, the Obscenity Unit threatened an endless litany of litigation against vendors of sexually oriented materials unless they agreed to plea bargains under which they gave up their First Amendment rights. The unit preferred plea agreements even to convictions because, through plea agreements, the government could force people to go out of business, whereas convictions punished them only for selling particular books or videos found to be obscene.

According to Edward Rosenthal, who defended one of the distributors against prosecutions in multiple districts, the unit "made clear to defendants that they would be prosecuted consecutively in multiple jurisdictions unless they agree to a guilty plea which would include their ceasing involvement with sexually explicit expressive materials," regardless of whether or not they could be declared obscene. In at least one case, the unit sought a plea agreement even before obtaining an indictment, but said it would withdraw the offer once the indictment was returned.

One of Project PostPorn's early targets was a company called Adult Entertainment Network. The company's owners eventually accepted a plea agreement under which they had to close their business and refrain permanently from disseminating any sexually explicit phone messages. The Obscenity Unit also threatened multi-district prosecution against Home Dish Only, a satellite network, and succeeded in obtaining a similar plea agreement prohibiting Home Dish from ever broadcasting "sexually oriented programming."

In a case against Toushin Company, a mail-order firm, the unit negotiated a plea bargain in which the defendants agreed to discontinue all business in the states of Tennessee and Utah. And the unit forced the owners of Panavue Enterprises, Inc., to accept a plea agreement to "terminate business operations," destroy or transfer all "sexually oriented" expressive material (including "artwork and advertising of a sexually oriented nature"), and never again "promote, produce, sell or distribute sexually oriented materials." In plea negotiations with "Adam & Eve" Company (a.k.a. PHE, Inc.) Ward and Lambert insisted that the company get out of the business of even "soft porn," including many R-rated videos, even though Ward acknowledged that such material was protected constitutionally. The prosecutors specified that the company would not be permitted to sell *Playboy*, *Penthouse*, or even marriage manuals like *The Joy of Sex*.

Nor did the unit limit its work to national distributors. In *U.S.* v. *Sial*, the unit used the threat of multiple federal and state prosecutions to shut down two adult movie theaters in Salt Lake City. According to Sial's lawyer, "If [Sial's owners] didn't close the theaters...there was a tax indictment that was going to come, and they would be indicted on the tax case. They would be indicted for RICO. They'd be indicted on federal obscenity charges, and they'd be indicted on state charges...and would be denaturalized and sent to Pakistan." Faced with this barrage of threatened prosecutions, Sial agreed to go out of business.

Three distributors tried to fight back. The target of at least five separate grand jury investigations, the owners of a mail-order company called Brussel/Pak Ventures sought an injunction against the unit's multiple-prosecution strategy. But Patrick Trueman, Showers's successor as head of the unit, threatened to prosecute them consecutively in at least five jurisdictions unless they agreed to cease any involvement with "sexually explicit materials." Even if they were acquitted in one or two cases, Trueman said, they would immediately be prosecuted in another jurisdiction until guilty verdicts were obtained. Karl Brussel, his wife, and his son were indicted in four separate jurisdictions and their trials were scheduled to begin at two-week intervals. Given these economic and personal pressures on family members, Brussel finally acquiesced: he pled guilty, agreed to go out of business, and he and his son gave up their First Amendment rights for their lifetimes. Brussel was sentenced to a year in prison, and his civil rights suit became moot.

Face with the prospect of defending prosecutions in Connecticut, Mississippi, Indiana, Delaware, and Utah, Avram Freedberg, a distributor of sexually oriented materials, obtained a civil injunction to protect himself. As in the Brussel case, the Justice Department indicted Freedberg and his wife. Lambert had told Freedberg's lawyer that he would be prosecuted simultaneously or consecutively in as many districts as necessary to obtain convictions. In the event all federal prosecutions resulted in acquittal, Lambert had said that Freedberg should be prepared to face state prosecutions, plus indictments of his employees and his wife. Nevertheless, a single Utah indictment and the government's continued efforts to overturn the injunction forced Freedberg to accept an agreement that he close his business and never again distribute sexually oriented materials. Because Freedberg accepted the agreement, the case has become moot.

Philip Harvey, the president of Adam & Eve, a mail-order distributor of sexually explicit materials, obtained a similar injunction after the unit tried to coerce him into a plea agreement that would have shut down his entire business, even though much of what he sold was merchandise, like lingerie and novelty items, none of which could be found obscene. Yet Showers believed that even these materials were unacceptable. "We are not willing to accept the kinds of materials that PHE distributes," he said.

The unit's subsequent plea demand was only slightly less restrictive. If Adam & Eve had agreed to it, it would not have been "free to even sell *Playboy* or *Penthouse* and it certainly meant [it] could not sell sexual manuals which are designed to aid couples, such as *The Joy of Sex*." Ward and Lambert made it clear that *any* depictions of nudity also would be prohibited.

When Adam & Eve's attorneys protested that these materials were clearly protected by the First Amendment, Ward and Lambert conceded the point. But the prosecutors made it clear, in the words of an Adam & Eve attorney, that it did not matter "if the entire congregation of the First Baptist Church of Plains, Georgia, would stand and vote that they are not obscene. If they are sexually oriented that is it." In July 1990, Washington D.C. federal judge Joyce Hens Green ruled that PHE had shown a substantial likelihood that the unit's conduct "constitute[d] bad faith calculated to suppress [Adam & Eve's] constitutional rights."

But Harvey's dealings with the unit are not over. It responded to the injunction by bringing federal obscenity charges against him in Utah. By Lambert's own admission, he proceeded to indict Harvey largely in response to Harvey's public criticism of the unit's actions.

Harvey and Adam & Eve are no stranger to the unit's tactics. In 1986–87, they had been subjected to simultaneous state and federal prosecutions in North Carolina. Justice Department officials had pressured state attorneys in North Carolina to bring obscenity charges against Harvey, but with little success. The prosecutor in Alamance County, North Carolina, did prosecute Harvey and Adam & Eve, but the jury deliberated for less than half an hour before acquitting them. Orange County, California, prosecutor Carl Fox refused to prosecute them at all, saying it would be "a total waste of time and law-enforcement resources."

The unit has not limited itself to the distributors of sexually oriented material. In the summer of 1990, it began multiple prosecutions against the Hollywood producers of adult videos. To ensure that these companies would not be tried in Los Angeles, where more liberal juries might acquit them, the unit set up phony video stores in conservative communities in Arkansas, Utah, Oklahoma, and North Carolina, and ordered tapes from the California companies.

The first producer to go on trial, a Hollywood company called Video Team, was convicted in Dallas in July 1991. But the judge rejected the government's attempt to seize all of the defendants' assets, noting that to destroy an entire business because of "*de minimis* use of the properties" to produce a few videos determined to be obscene by Dallas standards "serves no legitimate end; that is, no end other than destroying legal business enterprises simply because their stock and trade is sexually related materials."

In May 1991 the ACLU Arts Censorship Project filed a Freedom of Information Act (FOIA) request with the Department of Justice in an effort to learn more about the unit's activities and budget. Although the FOIA requires that the government respond to requests for information within ten days, the Department of Justice has thus far failed to furnish any of the requested information—a failure which may necessitate the filing of a lawsuit. The unit's reported annual budget in 1990 was $1.7 million, but the figure does not reflect the vast sums of money being spent on these prosecutions which are hidden in the budgets of U.S. Attorneys' offices throughout the country. Although we do not yet have hard figures, it is clear that the government is spending millions of dollars in taxpayers' money to put these distributors out of business, and that the cost of these prosecutions far outstrips the amount given in grants by the National Endowment for the Arts that has occupied so much of the public's attention in the past year.

Dangerous Fallout from the Justice Department's Crusade

A clear risk posed by the Obscenity Unit is that it may contribute to the creation of a climate of fear and intimidation for any artist or arts organization that becomes involved with work containing sexually explicit elements. There is at least preliminary evidence that the Obscenity Unit's activities have coincided with stepped-up scattershot enforcement actions nationwide against non-obscene literature, art, theater, and film that involve nudity or treat sexual themes. The Obscenity Unit's activities have also occurred simultaneous with intensified efforts to ban books in public schools and libraries and to restrict the National Endowment for the Arts.

For example, police in the town of Norwood, Massachusetts, visited several video stores early in 1991, threatening to prosecute the owners unless they removed all adult videotapes from their shelves. The officers did not specify which movies they thought were obscene, nor had they viewed any of the videos. The ACLU filed suit against the town and eventually succeeded in halting the unconstitutional practice, but not before several distributors had agreed to give up their First Amendment rights to rent and sell non-obscene adult films. Moreover, prosecutors in other parts of the country have been undeterred by the Norwood suit. Law-enforcement authorities in Georgia, Iowa, Ohio, Pennsylvania, Nebraska, and other states have threatened to bring obscenity prosecutions against distributors who rent or sell "X-rated," NC-17-rated, and even unrated videos.

The atmosphere created by the National Obscenity Enforcement Unit's practices has affected other art forms as well. In Cincinnati, Ohio, state prosecutors tried to shut down an exhibit of internationally acclaimed photographer Robert Mapplethorpe's work by charging the director of the Contemporary Arts Center with obscenity. City governments in North Carolina and Tennessee have sought to ban productions of the Broadway musical *Oh! Calcutta!* And last year officials in

Charlotte, North Carolina, refused to allow the staging of Terrence McNally's play *Frankie and Johnny in the Claire de Lune* unless the producers excised nudity from the production. More and more frequently, artworks with simple nudity are being banned from college campuses and public schools. And last year in Florida, for the first time, a musical recording—by the 2 Live Crew rap group—was declared obscene by a local judge.

Perhaps the most egregious case, though, involved the April 1990 raid by FBI agents and San Francisco police on the home of noted art photographer Jock Sturges, who has taken many non-pornographic photographs of children in the nude with their parents' permission. The agents ransacked Sturges' apartment and seized hundreds of thousands of his photo negatives and thousands of photographic prints (most not even nudes), as well as his personal papers, address books, business records, computer and photographic equipment, passport, a copy of Vladimir Nabokov's *Lolita*, and several art books; and held them for more than ten months despite his attorney's many requests for their return. After a massive international investigation—including interrogation of art-gallery owners and demands for their customer lists—and a lengthy presentation to a federal grand jury in the spring of 1991, the grand jury ultimately refused to indict Sturges. But the damage to Sturges's career had been done. His ability to function as a commercial photographer was seriously impaired by the seizure of his equipment and records, and the government's continuing accusations that he was a child pornographer.

When the government finally returned Sturges's equipment, some of it was badly damaged. About eighty percent of his commercial negatives were returned smudged or ruined. Police wrote "no porn seen" in heavy black marker across the bindings in which the negatives were kept. "It's government graffiti, a lasting sign of their presence," Sturges mused.

The real losers in this battle, however, will not be just pornographers, raunchy rap musicians, or artists who deal with sexual themes. Rather, the losers will be the American people. Sexual themes have been an integral part of art and culture since the beginning of civilization. The Supreme Court has rightly described sex as "a great and mysterious motive force in human life that has indisputably been a subject of absorbing interest to mankind throughout the ages; it is one of the vital problems of human interest and public concern."

The chilling effect of the Justice Department's campaign has seeped beyond the already-dim boundaries separating obscenity from art. Filmmakers, novelists, sculptors, and photographers alike feel constrained by the self-appointed censor's repressive actions and by the atmosphere of cultural conformity and fear they have fostered.

Conclusion

A national unit to wipe out obscenity is fundamentally flawed because it is incongruent with the Supreme Court's definition of legal obscenity. The community standards test first enunciated by the Court in its 1973 decision *Miller* v. *California* requires that prosecution of obscenity take place at the local level, if at all. The Court created the community standard test for two reasons. First, so that the people of Maine or Mississippi would not have to "accept public depiction of conduct found tolerable in Las Vegas or New York City"; and second, so that less-restrictive standards in some communities are not "strangled by the absolutism of imposed uniformity."

But by choosing to bring charges in conservative communities like Utah and North Carolina, the unit has sought to prohibit sexually oriented material nationwide by using the lowest common denominator. The result is that communities that find such material inoffensive are deprived of access to them. Moreover, the record shows that this unit has been on a crusade to suppress as much sexually oriented art and information as possible, even depictions of the human body.

Most disturbing of all, history has shown that obscenity prosecutions punish and suppress works of enduring literary and artistic value. They have also impeded access to important information concerning sexuality and birth control. The renowned feminist Margaret Sanger was once harassed and prosecuted for obscenity because she advocated the legalization of birth control. Literary classics like D. H. Lawrence's *Lady Chatterley's Lover,* James Joyce's *Ulysses,* Henry Miller's *Tropic of Cancer* and many other great works of literature and art have in the past been refused entry to the United States, or have been prosecuted and suppressed. It is the same impulse to impose a particular and narrow sensibility on everyone else that animates the work of the National Obscenity Enforcement Unit. This is precisely the impulse that the First Amendment was meant to deter.

Recommendations

The American Civil Liberties Union recommends the following:

That the National Obscenity Enforcement Unit/Child Exploitation and Obscenity Section be disbanded by the United States Attorney General or the President.

That Congress, in the interim, conduct oversight hearings to monitor the unit's activities and ensure that they remain within constitutional bounds.

RAW:
AN INTERVIEW WITH ART SPIEGELMAN
Doug Martin

....

In 1983 Art Spiegelman's *Raw* was in its infancy. The highly acclaimed comic was published in a repressive era as regards adult comics. With the threat of pornography raids hanging over comic stores, there was the possibility a store would stock *Raw* and be busted. While *Raw*'s editors would not be affected directly, they felt it unfair for comic stores to face such a threat. As a result, in *Raw # Five* the editors blocked out "private parts" of the "Theodore Death Head" strip. The issue's opening editorial proclaimed, "Self-censorship is the better part of valor for publishers trying to keep local distributors and retailers out of trouble." The editors did make available paste-on stickers by mail for readers to "clip and stick in the privacy of their own homes." In this exclusive interview for *Gauntlet,* Art Spiegelman looks back on the controversy.

G: What is the general concept behind *Raw*?
AS: Essentially to function as a showcase for a certain slice of what's possible in comics internationally.

G: What is its audience?
AS: Beats me. We've never designed it for an audience. Ultimately, the audience is me and a few other people I know. It's done sort of abstractly in the sense of, well, let's just put out what we think is the best. Whatever that is, it gets to the magazine with the assumption that somebody might be interested in seeing the best comics.

G: Why did you decide to delete the penises from the "Theodore Death Head" issue?
AS: Well, it seemed that at the time [1983] there had been some rumblings of pornography busts in comic shops. At that time a lot of our distribution was through comic-book stores, and we couldn't control which ones would get it or where. It was going through several comic distributors, and it seemed somewhat irresponsible to get stores carrying *Raw* busted in that there wasn't a climate like there had been a few years earlier, when I was involved with underground comics that would understand, justify, and accept "hard-core comics." It didn't seem that we would be affected directly, but it did seem very possible that some comic shop somewhere might get busted and have to go through all this crap because they had some comics that had penetration shots in them.

So maybe there was more discretion than necessary. It's hard to judge. We figured we should try to find a solution to this. One was to try to put "adults only" or "X-rated" and put it in a bag or something that didn't seem enticing. What seemed more interesting was to find a solution that would have its own elegance once we had defined the problem the way we had. And this particular idea of overtly blocking out penises that are the size of lampposts called attention to the fact that we were doing it and could make it an issue. It seemed that if we could do this, in a way that was so overt and actually make some kind of statement about the climate of the time, then we could turn the whole thing into a game by providing the actual penises that you could cut apart and put in. The gamelike quality of making it into a kid's sticker book was very much in keeping with the artist's sensibility. So it kind of added to—rather than detracted from—the comic. It wasn't censorship in the sense of deprivation, it was censorship turned against itself to create something more energetic than it might have been originally.

G: Was it a promotional gimmick?
AS: That has nothing to do with it. We're just trying to do things that are provocative and interesting.

G: Do you feel the climate has changed since you put out that specific issue?
AS Yeah. I think it has simultaneously gotten more uptight and more open. The climate of the country at large has gotten incredibly uptight. On the other hand, within publishing itself, I'd say that more things can happen now than in '83. It may lead to some kind of crackdown again, but at the moment comic books are moving much more toward being a kind of hardcore sexual—erotic at best—pornography. There's a lot more of that kind of product in stores these days.

G: So you feel the sexual nature of comics nowadays is overdone?
AS: Well, I think it's overdone in the sense that it's the same old thing. Most of the stuff I've seen is neither a real turn-on for me, nor is it really breaking new turf. It's like there it is again. Come shots and goo dripping down female lips. Nothing against either activity, but in the same old depiction it has more to do with people's repression than with people's liberation. It's sorta feeding off the fact that people are so tense.

G: If the need arose, would you censor yourself again?
AS: Well, if I perceived it as a need I certainly would. In '83 I

perceived it as a sort of kindness multiplied into a creative act. A kindness toward those bookstores that would be getting into trouble because of the way pornography laws are enforced. Certainly the audience wouldn't get into trouble and *Raw* wouldn't really get into trouble. But some store out there would have its hands full for having carried our magazine.

In term of needs, now, I would say that I and every other artist censors every day they work one way or another. That's part of the process. Whether you are censoring out sentimental, virtuous thoughts in order to make your work down and nasty, or whether you're censoring out the most base and unacceptable parts of yourself in order to appeal to a certain set of values. No matter where you are coming from, work does involve a certain canceling out of parts. That's what's shaping us. When you shape something, you're getting rid of something else, pushing it into a certain form.

G: What is the problem with erotic comics of today?
AS: What I object to in a lot of comics I'm seeing is that they're really banal. They're not as imaginative as my own masturbatory fantasies. They just ritualize them; they make sex boring.

G: In defining censorship, what is considered obscene and what is considered art?
AS: I'm not sure it's necessary to differentiate between the two. I think that all this stuff tends to sort itself out. It's not a matter of outlawing it ultimately. I'm a First Amendment absolutist, so it seems to me that as horrible as some of today's stuff is, it's just a reflection that people's heads are filled with horrible junk. And the best that one can do is to offer alternative ends to it; just assume there may be some possibility of change in which repression won't be so severe.

But I don't believe censoring does anything except create more of that bottled-up tension. There's something really pathetic about it. I live right off Canal Street in New York and we've got three stores that sell only X-rated videos and the whole neighborhood is up in arms about it. It doesn't seem that the way to deal with it is by closing up those shops.

G: What with the Mapplethorpe controversy and the trial of the museum director in Cincinnati, do you think we in America will execute poets the way the Russians once did?

AS: We don't have to execute our poets. All we have to do is starve them. You just make it a lot more lucrative to become [a servant to corporate interests]. I don't think it will go as far as executing artists. If we ever start executing artists it won't be the ones who make work of sexual content, it will be the ones who make work of political contention.

On the other hand, the sexual repression we have sucks. It has to do with all the insane homophobia and this kind of wrapping ourselves up in our little flags. Just the worst of what America has to offer. All of this NEA stuff seems like a replay of George Bush's flag-waving election speeches. The reaction to Mapplethorpe and the crucifixion-in-urine photo is all a version of wrapping oneself in the flag.

G: What do you think is the greatest threat to comics in contemporary America?

AS: Probably the banality of the interrelations between the artist and the audience, because there's an audience that really wants one kind of thing. And there's a number of artists who make that kind of thing. The biggest threat to any flourishing of comics is that the audience doesn't ask for very much. Therefore, artists don't provide very much. The standards are pretty low.

G: It's more commercial than artistic, then?

AS: I'm talking about trying to make art, but the demand, desire, or even receptivity to real arts and comics is not very widespread. What people really want from comics is really something else. There's a threat implicit in making art and an audience willing to take the dare is small. But despite this fact, somehow or other, there are copies of *Raw* getting out.

Copies of *Raw* can be ordered through Raw Books and Graphics, 27 Greene Street, New York, NY 10013, or at most comic stores.

CHERI GAULKE:
PERFORMANCE ARTIST UNDER ATTACK

William Relling, Jr.

A list of the accomplishments and commendations of Los Angeles–based artist Cheri Gaulke would fill more than a dozen pages. Since earning her BFA from the Minneapolis College of Art and Design in 1975, she has been at the forefront of the avant-garde feminist art movement. She is also an environmental activist of renown—a founding member of the antinuclear performance art group Sisters of Survival [S.O.S.] that, from 1981 through 1985, toured throughout the United States and Europe. However, it is as a solo artist that Gaulke came to the attention of Senator Jesse Helms and others who have expressed opposition to her work. (A performance in Santa

Monica in 1990 titled, "Hey Jesse! You Ain't Seen Nothin' Yet!" was her response.) Recently Gaulke spoke with her high-school classmate, writer William Relling Jr., on the subjects of Senator Helms, feminism, history, religion, politics, and censorship.

G: Getting right into the political content of your work, I understand you were accosted recently by Jesse Helms. [Gaulke laughs.] If not personally, then certainly through the media. Tell me about that.
CG: Basically, my name appeared in the paper one day, in the *Village Voice*, that I was an artist who was doing this kind of "blasphemous" artwork.

G: Was it in connection with a specific piece of work?
CG: It was partly "This is My Body," partly "Virgin." They were kind of confused about exactly what they were pinpointing, because their information was a little garbled. They objected to my portraying the serpent, Eve, Jesus Christ, a witch in performances, in "This is My Body," where I did all that. I'd described, in a press release, the performance being part Christian worship service, part pagan ritual. They objected to that. I'd done another piece about artificial insemination, where I played the Virgin Mary reading a book, *How to Have a Baby without a Man*, and the angel Gabriel appearing to her and saying, "Try artificial insemination." That was also depicted [in the article].

I wrote about [Helms] in a statement for a performance I did in England [in the fall of 1991], and I was thinking that in some ways I was flattered to be noticed. Somehow it meant that my message had gotten through. That here I'd been critiquing Christianity's attitudes about sexuality, particularly *female* sexuality for years, and people in politics [finally] noticed.

G: What's the symbolism behind Eve eating the apple in "This is My Body"?
CG: Eve eating the apple, in Christian history, has been held up to women as the first woman who was responsible for the demise of humankind. My use of the image is to be critical of Christianity

saying that. Eating the apple is a metaphor—a woman exploring her sexuality which gets to be taboo [in Christianity].

G: You were also criticized for your depiction of a woman on a cross in "Passion." What caused the flap there?
CG: I was portraying a priest or a monk, and I took off my robes and climbed up on the cross. The projection of Jesus merges with my body, and I began to feel the pain of the choice of putting myself on the cross. This was the first performance where I put myself on the cross—which became a controversial statement, being sort of a female Christ. News articles objected to the fact that I portrayed myself as Christ.

G: How did it come to Helms's attention specifically?
CG: I think some conservative reporter did research and decided to pinpoint particular artists, then brought it to Helms to bolster his efforts to cut funding for the NEA, funding for the arts. I began to realize that it wasn't really about me, it wasn't really about my work. I was just grist for the mill. I was just being used to further his campaign.

G: What sort of pressure did he put on you?
CG: I read in the paper that he asked the General Accounting Office of Congress to do an investigation of my work [because] I received an NEA grant in 1983. But no one ever contacted me personally. Later I was audited [by the IRS], which I thought may or may not have been a coincidence.

That's what's so weird, being aware of all these people talking *about* you, but they never talk *to* you. So you never get to really…"defend" myself isn't the right word. You never get to set the record straight. Talk about blaspheming. They're taking *my* name in vain, presenting my work out of context. They're manipulating the emotions of readers, of the public. It's really a cheap shot. Anybody can do that. And it's full of lies.

G: What are your feelings about the relationship between religion and politics? My take on what you do is that it's quite religious, in the sense that there's a spirituality to it, there's a connection to some higher power by whatever name you want to call it—Nature or God. Am I wrong about that?

CG: No, you're very right. "Higher power" maybe isn't a [phrase] I would use, because I think I'm more into reclaiming the sacredness within myself and within you and within all beings and all matter. What I think happens in Christianity is that it's very separated from *us*. It's on the outside of us, and we try to attain [salvation]. And of course [Christianity] teaches that we'll never attain it as long as we're in our bodies, because our bodies are flesh and they're evil, and they have sexual desires. So therefore we must repress them and put them down. That for me is very dangerous. What seems spiritual and profound—this belief in God as some higher thing to attain—to me is ultimately extremely dangerous because it justifies violence. Ultimately it justifies violence against women, against nature, this whole idea of "dominion" over. Rather than seeing that, in fact, we are within nature, we are part of it, we're not separate from it.

[For example] with the whole nuclear issue, I began to realize how ludicrous the idea of destroying the planet was. It's so human—ego invested—because *we* could never destroy the planet. We're just like ants. We're these little, puny, vulnerable creatures. We'll destroy ourselves. We'll destroy the planet's ability to feed us or sustain our lives because *we're* so fragile. But the *planet* will continue. The planet, whether you want to call it a goddess or some kind of life form or Nature in the larger, cosmic sense—there's no way we could destroy it.

This has gone off on a tangent here a little. But the connection between religion and politics...lately I've been doing some research. The so-called "Founding Fathers" of our country were not Christians, contrary to what people like Jerry Falwell and Jesse Helms would like you to believe. They were deists. Which is really humanistic and more where I'm coming from.

G: I suppose if you've read Benjamin Franklin's *Autobiography* or stuff that Thomas Jefferson wrote, you could arrive at that conclusion.

CG: There's documented stuff about it. "So help me God," the pledge you take in court? Any kind of swearing of allegiance?

That is not actually required. I didn't know that until just recently. Our so-called "Founding Fathers" were into keeping church and state separate. Essentially, the Supreme Court is there to be the arbiter between them. What really concerns me is the ways in which people like Falwell and Helms are trying to reconnect those two and equate patriotism with belief in God.

When I read Margaret Atwood's *The Handmaid's Tale,* that to me was the most powerful book. To me it was the feminist *1984,* because it's really my worst fear about where we're heading, in terms of complete enslavement of women. Our only value to this patriarchal culture is that we reproduce. [Atwood's book] may be a paranoid extreme, but I feel like I've seen that happen in history. In the Middle Ages something like nine million people—mostly women—were killed [as witches]. This went on for hundreds of years, this incredible...ludicrous... it's just laughable, the things they were accused of. [Things like] "removing a male member." Women were completely scapegoated. There were some villages where every single woman was put to death. What's scary to me is not only did that happen, but that no one talks about it anymore. It's not something that we learn about in history class—it's just like neo-Nazis who say the Holocaust didn't happen. To me that's very scary when the culture loses the history of oppression. We lose the lessons that we learned through those things.

G: So the danger in mixing religion and politics is what?
CG: Politics is the enforcer. Religion doesn't have the power to put someone to death or in prison. They need the state to do that. That was the perfect marriage they had going in the Middle Ages. It was a very profit-making industry. A lot of people had the job of locking women up and recording the trials and being the jury. Apparently there were all these different jobs: the job of getting her, taking her from her house. The job of feeding her in jail. The job of bringing her to the courtroom. And guess who paid for it? *She* did. Because they seized her property, and they divided the spoils, and it paid the expenses. God, what a brilliant capitalist concept! [Laughs.] It was an incredible racket.

G: Are there parallels to things going on today?

CG: There are some rackets coming down nowadays. I think what's happening with abortion being threatened is really, really frightening. That's a case where women have [in the past] and will [in the future] lose their lives. To have the freedom to make that choice...such blatant disregard for a woman's sense of her own body, her integrity, her own desires and needs is really what I feel is behind it.

G: Do you find it curious that a lot of these leaders of anti-abortion groups are male?
CG: Along with an occasional Phyllis Schlafly. It's not to say that women are superior to men, or that all men are fucked. I don't believe that at all. But it is clear to me who has power in this society, and it's not women.

G: Any number of social critics have referred to where we are now—"we" meaning society—as "postfeminist." What's your take on that?
CG: At first I hated that term because it felt like a put-down to the feminist movement. That somehow we were talking beyond it all, which I really don't think we are. Now I understand it more as a historical term, in terms of meaning that "feminism" as an organized movement doesn't really exist in the way that it did in the 60s and 70s. But I know that feminism is alive and well in the hearts of many women *and* men. I just don't think there's a national strategy.

One of the reasons for that, one of the problems of any kind of movement—[not just] feminism—is that desire to distill a diverse group of people into having a small set of needs and demands. When, in fact, who women are is an extremely diverse cross section of our society. Women are of different races, different classes. Our needs and our issues are very different. That's where feminism broke down.

G: Do you think the current relationship between religion and politics is a reaction to feminism as a movement in the 60s and 70s?
CG: When women get strong, is there a backlash? Is that the question?

G: Yes.
CG: I think that could have something to do with it. When women start to get organized, yeah, I think there is a backlash. In the Middle Ages, apparently, in the period preceding the witch burnings, there were more women than men. Men were getting killed off by wars, and—this is what I heard one historian say—to some of the plagues, some of the diseases, men were more susceptible than women. So there were more women than men. It meant that women were surviving their husbands, and women were owning more property, that sort of thing. That's interesting to me. [So the men say:] "Okay, we got to *do* something about this! They're outta control!" [Laughs.]

I guess I see history as being two parts. I see this kind of pre-Christian part of history, which women in the past few years have been trying to reclaim. This whole "goddess" movement, which is not a new thing. It's documented that there were thousands and thousands of years during which people existed in cooperation with nature. There was a pantheon of gods and goddesses that were symbolic or metaphoric of cycles of nature. Some people [have suggested] that it was a matriarchal society, [but] I feel uncomfortable with the term "matriarchal," because I think it implies that women ruled over men. I prefer "matristic," a sort of "woman-centered" culture. But it's clear that [at that time] the female body was respected and worshipped as reflecting the cycles of nature. The difficulty about reclaiming that part of our history is that it's largely oral tradition. It's before the written word, for the most part. But there are objects, and there are ruins which have been found.

Then what you have is a shift in power, to patriarchy. At that point, the people with power rewrote the story. So when you look at something like the Garden of Eden, and you have this cast of characters—the evil snake, the tree with fruit on it, the sexual woman who's listening to the snake and eating the fruit—you realize, in fact, it's pre-Christian symbolism. In ancient Egypt, they worshiped Hathor, the goddess of the tree. They believed that the tree was her body, and that she handed out fruit to the dead, which was her gift of eternal life. Serpents were kept in temples, and they whispered to the priestesses, and so on. With the shift to patriarchy, the stories had to be rewritten—the fairy tales, the definitions of what is "erotic," the laws.

That's why for me there are two phases of history. The earlier phase is when the flesh and the spirit were not thought of as divided. In other words, the—matter was sacred. To have a physical presence did not imply carnality and weakness. But after this changed, the flesh and the spirit became divided. The spirit became valued over the flesh, and somehow men, since they were writing the rules, got to be more spiritual than women. Men were the only ones who could officiate and be ministers.

What I saw [for example] when I read [the Book of] Revelations is this story of Jesus coming down as a great warrior to fight the Great Whore of Babylon—who gets to portray the matter, the flesh, the world is this big slut! [Laughs.] Again, it's that desire to destroy the flesh, to destroy nature, to destroy women.

G: I know that censorship is an issue you've had some ambivalence about in the past, in terms of how it relates to pornography. You were involved with an anti-pornography movement for a while, weren't you?

CG: Within the feminist movement, in the 70s, there was a targeting of pornography and violence against women. There was a group called Women Against Violence in Pornography and Media. They held a conference in San Francisco [in which] I was involved as an artist. Bringing a group of women up there for performances and stuff.

I think what was going on then was really important, [because] it was raising the issue of does pornography lead to violence. There are all sorts of questions about that. [As a consequence] things have changed a lot. I think more women are involved in pornography, in terms of being the creators and not just the... I don't know if "victims" is the right word. Not just the ones whose bodies are being used.

One of the dangers of what was happening at that time is this discussion of whether to legislate pornography. Should pornography be outlawed, or is pornography freedom of expression? I see how it doesn't really work to legislate it. They could legislate me just as easily. It's very easy for people like Helms and Falwell to say that *I'm* pornographic and my work is obscene. I think there needs to be an awareness of the issues in terms of whether a person is being used or abused. I'm not crazy about violence but I certainly feel people have a right to [explore] violence artistically. I'm not particularly aesthetically attracted to violence, although I can be pretty graphic in my performances about violence that's been committed, because I want people to know about that.

G: Is there such a thing as obscenity for you? Is there such a thing as pornography?
CG: I don't know if I have a "limit" as far as obscenity goes. Certainly I have limits in terms of what is personally offensive to me. But it's like the discussion about is there such a thing as "evil." I really don't think there is. I really don't believe in evil. I think "evil" [like obscenity] is something that's defined by one group to use against another group. Since I happen to be in the group that it usually gets used against, whether that be women or even artists or homosexuals, I see the danger in that.

It's so hard to define it. I feel there is a responsibility to protect people who can't protect themselves, like young people. But then you get into people [who] say the unborn are people who can't protect themselves. *That* can be used against you, too. Or the elderly. [Anything] can be used as a way of taking someone else's power.

It's like Bret Easton Ellis's book *American Psycho*. There were some feminist groups calling for a boycott of that book. I think that's fine. I boycott Coors. If the workers are striking Corona, I'll boycott Corona. To me that's freedom of expression. But I don't think that [Ellis's book] should be banned or outlawed. He should have every right to write that book and publish it. Bookstores have the right to sell it. I would fight for that right.

G: You're planning a new performance for May. Have you self-censored yourself, or don't you care how you are perceived? Does the threat of persecution hang over your head?

CG: Yes, I'm always thinking about it. I do have nudity in my new performance, but all of it is behind a scrim, which I've never done before. Now is that because I am putting a layer between myself and the audience? Is that a kind of veiled censorship? I don't know. Or is it purely an aesthetic thing? I'm trying not to self-censor, but I am certainly aware of the inner debate.

G: Do you have any fear of being targeted because of he sexual or controversial nature of your performance art?
CG: Yes, I do. It's a funny double-edged sword. On the one hand, one gets a lot of visibility for being controversial, and I find in some ways I've benefited by having the finger pointed at me. On the other hand, I've seen artists, who have been more involved in this debate than I have, pay dearly on a personal level. Having to spend so much time fighting those battles can be frustrating and exhausting emotionally. I so identify historically with the witch-burning period that I fear persecution. I anticipate it in some ways. I do feel, though, that I will be true to what I think is the most important and best image to do in my work: what is best, not work that's safest. I'm a mature artist. I've been doing this stuff for almost twenty years, so the decisions I make are tempered with experience. I sort of trust my judgment; and if I feel unsure of myself, I'll consult with other people who have this experience.

G: Is the climate today more repressive than several years ago? Would your earlier performance pieces, for example, have stirred more controversy if done today?
CG: Yes. People are sort of looking for it in a way they weren't looking before. There is a concerted effort by special-interest groups to push down women, certainly minorities and gays.

G: Why do you think these are more repressive times?
CG: I see the economy having a lot to do with it. People feel insecure. There's a feeling there's not enough to go around, so the power groups want to make sure they get their part. That's why David Duke has been so successful. He's tapping into middle-class white people's fear of not getting what they perceive as their

share. There's a perception that women or minorities have more power.

G: How do you combat this?
CG: It's important to keep on doing the work we've been doing. We can't shrink back into the closet and be timid. We have to continue to be aggressive and be aggressive in a responsible way—not do things just for shock value.

"BOILED" DIANA

Scott Cunningham

Underground publications, by definition, touch on topics of transgressions whether they be sexual, political, philosophical, or artistic. Often it's a blend of all four. The "self" in self-publishing is the yin to the yang of "self-censorship." Self-publishing is the only way to guarantee complete control over your own material. By putting out your own 'zine you can beat the inherent checks and balances built into commercially driven mainstream publishing. And now with the rise of "political correctness" one more nail goes into the coffin of free speech. Almost everyone who does self-publish loses money and wastes valuable TV-watching time; their measly rewards coming in occasional fan letters or positive reviews in other 'zines. So imagine the hell of going through tedious production work to grind out your occasional effort, and your prize is jail time. It could happen in the case of Mike Diana, poor white trash from the Sunshine State, whose little digest of comics and stories may put him behind bars.

Mike Diana works at his dad's convenience store in Largo, Florida, selling cigarettes and beer to the drunks and crack-heads who wander into the place looking like wasted cannibals from the gory zombie movies he loves. Until recently, he used to go home to the trailer in which he lived with his younger brother and draw comics every night. But when the news of his indictment hit the papers, there were some problems with the police, and the people who were letting him stay there asked him to leave. Mike's a twenty-two year old artist and an enemy of the state—at least the state of Florida. And I guess that means I am, too, since I have contributed work to his magazine ever since I met him—through the mail—in 1989, curating a show on 'zines. There were hundreds of publications in the exhibit, lots of them exploring sexually deviate themes; but somehow Mike's comic *Angel Fuck* (now renamed *Boiled Angel* because of trouble with the Post Office over the f-word in the title) remained the strongest in my memory, simply because it was so extreme. It's as if all the evil and nasty images vomited forth by underground '60s id-monsters like Rory Hayes and S. Clay Wilson had been concentrated and combined with the pop violence of contemporary gore movies and the minimal lyrics of hard-core punk music. Drawn in a primitive style of glorified high-school doodles, Mike's work has an obsessive urgency that undercuts its cynical, flat humor. A typical Mike Diana story starts with a young boy excited to hear that he's finally been adopted, then immediately being beaten and raped by his new father once they are alone. The boy winds up slaving away at his evil stepdad's factory, grinding up babies for dog food. He eventually kills stepdaddy, but the abuse doesn't stop there. The boy's dog ends up raping him. ("Oh, no, Spot! Not you, too!")

In the land of the free and the home of the brave, Mike has managed to cross the line again and again. His work dealing with child abuse, sex, murder, torture, and Satanism has, over the years I've known him, turned *Boiled Angel* into a magnet of controversy. Whenever comic shops are raided, *Boiled Angel* always heads the list of obscene materials confiscated. In 1990 Mike became a suspect in the FBI's investigation into a Gainesville serial killer *simply because of the material he was printing*—no other evidence was necessary for the Bureau to question him and order a blood test. Recently, Last Gasp, one of the biggest alternative distributors around, refused to reorder *Run Ron*, a successfully selling title, because Mike's strip had drawn such strong complaints (though Tower Books should be commended for continuing to sell *Run Ron* and *Boiled Angel*). When you think about it, the Florida indictment seemed destined; though it's strange it would come down now, since it's been over a year and a half ago that the last issue of *Boiled Angel* appeared.

But then who can figure Florida, anyway? The same state that brought you the 2 Live Crew trial now has decided to boost Mike's career by attacking his First Amendment rights. And there may be no escape from Florida's moralistic goosestep, now that Dade County's own Janet Reno is calling the shots for the whole country. An eye-popping story about her being a secret right-wing nut case was exposed in Alexander Cockburn's column for *The Nation* in April 1993. He recounts her trumped-up case against a fifteen-year-old boy accused of child molestation, revealing her demonization of a totally innocent kid. After reading that article, I couldn't help thinking about Reno's move to attack the Branch Davidian complex because of rumors of child abuse (still just rumors, I might point out) and you can see a pattern: as soon as there's a whiff of possible child abuse, individual rights literally go up in smoke. Reno's motto—"We had to kill the children to save them"—may become this country's idea of justice for the next few years.

Florida's Assistant State Attorney Stuart Baggish states: "The First Amendment was framed and built for the benefit of society. It was never contemplated for the protection of obscene materials the contents of which weaken the moral fiber of society. That's why we'll all be asking for jail time—the maximum punishment." If found guilty of three misdemeanor charges for producing lewd and obscene material, Mike could be sentenced to three years in jail and fined $3,000. His case has been taken up with the Comic Book Legal Defense Fund, and his trial date is due to be set during a hearing before a judge in late July. If you want to write Mike in support, or beg him for copies of the infamous issues 7 and 8 of *Boiled Angel*—now state's evidence in the case—he can be contacted at: P.O. Box 5254, Largo, FL 34649. To see his most recent work available, check out Issue 19 of *World War 3 Illustrated,* Issue 3 of *Snake Eyes,* and Issue 8 of *The Brutarian.*

JOE COLEMAN
AN INTERVIEW
Carlo McCormick

••••••••••••••••••••••••••••••••

Editor's note: Performance and comic artist Joe Coleman was born to be in hot water. Along the way, he has offended animal rights activists, the MPAA, and thought-control police…to name just a few. What's more, he couldn't care less. Taking his opposition in stride, he has even incorporated attempts to disrupt and stifle his work into his performance art—with startling results. He is an artist who works to please himself; whether others are amused, enthralled, or outraged is immaterial. His philosophy and art are revealed in this interview by New York writer Carlo McCormick.

G: Most of the problems you've encountered, in terms of censorship, have been as a performer and not so much for your work as a visual artist.
JC: I've had some censorship with the comics, too. For instance, in a recent issue of *Blab,* which has an interview with me and a comic strip I did on Carl Panzram on the cover, that comic you see is not the original cover, which was "The couple that slays together stays together," and was censored. Dennis Kitchen didn't want to print it because he though his distributor would not pick it up. Another case that was mentioned before in *Gauntlet* was the painting that I did for the film *Henry: Portrait of a Serial Killer.* It was supposed to be the movie poster and was commissioned by the director of the film, John McNaughton, but the distributor prevented it. Instead they did a new poster that's very similar, except that it's a photograph instead of my artwork.

G: In both instances, it's a case of self-censorship, out of fear, rather than any outside voice of authority actually interceding in the project.
JC: Yeah, it was them coming to me, asking me to do something, and then thinking that it was too strong.

G: This sort of self-censorship within the "creative" community has become increasingly prevalent as an alarming trend in the arts today. However, it's been your work as a performance artist that's been subject to direct censorship of people in authority trying to stop, or persecute you for your shows.
JC: Yeah, that's almost like part of the performance now. It's gotten to the point where I do the show, but then the show itself has a life of its own and tells me a story that I didn't even plan. One of the earliest ones which is really full of irony is the famous movie trial here in New York, where Bob Barker had me arrested for eating mice. What's incredible about it is the guy's name is Barker, which is slang for the sideshow pitchman who would introduce freak acts. One of the most famous freaks is the geek, and here he is coming out in the press saying, "Here's this horrible man that eats live rats," just like a barker would do. The

guy's a real classic barker, too, because he does TV shows like *Truth or Consequences* in which he exploits people's greed by making them do the most humiliating things in order to win stupid prizes. Then he refused to be the host of the Miss America pageant, which he'd done for a long time, because they were wearing fur coats. But meanwhile, their advertisers, like all those cosmetic companies, systematically use animal by-products, so it's kind of phony at the same time.

G: Bob Barker became aware of you through your part in the movie *Mondo New York*. Didn't that film have distribution problems because of its content?

JC: That was one of the first that had that rating problem, which *Henry* also had. Both were released unrated, because if they'd been released with one it would have been an X, and those days it wasn't like in the 60s or 70s where movies like *Clockwork Orange* were rated X, but still played all the theaters. You can't play an X-rated film at a normal theater these days, which cuts out your distribution. Some of my performance nights, like the one in Boston, have been real interesting in the way that events surrounding the shows transform them into something else. That show, which was pretty personal to begin with, had to do with my mother's death, which occurred just four days before it. She died of cancer and had been suffering from it for a long time. The performance was sort of a tribute to her, starting out with my collection of old, grainy pornographic films of fucking and sucking from some unidentifiable period of old hard-core pornography.

After about twenty minutes, the lights came on, and I burst through the screen hanging upside down from a cable, swinging over the audience, screaming and exploding. Fucking and sucking is what created me, from some time in the distant past; that's what my parents were doing. Here I am exploding—I thought the Big Bang theory of creation was the appropriate one—and hanging from the ceiling because you come into the world upside down attached to an umbilical cord.

There was also a goat—the placenta, hanging upside down next to me. The explosions were extinguished with cow's blood.

After the rope was cut, I went into the audience, sat with them, and introduced them to Mommy and Daddy. In this case, they were two rats I had christened Mommy and Daddy.

I bit off the head of Daddy because I had a lot of problems with my father; but I swallowed my mother, and that has a lot to do with my Christian background—eating the body and drinking the blood of Christ. When my mother met my father, she was excommunicated, and her priest, who she was really into, told her she was going to burn in Hell for all eternity because you were not allowed, at that time in the Catholic church, to get a divorce. She was so afraid of Hell, she denied her death until the end, and just would not accept that she was going to die.

So then I set off all the fires in the theater, the fires of Hell. The effigy of me was on fire. Everything started exploding, the place filled with smoke, and all the fire alarms went off. That's what brought the fire department there. The biggest thing they charged me with was "possession of an infernal machine." That's something that I never intended to put into it—something the outside world picked up and made into its own thing. Whether it has to do with legend, with Jules Verne, or whatever, it's like what Barker did: it's like I'm playing a game with my life. I'm doing things, then the world does things back to me, and then I react to it.

G: You had similar problems with the authorities when you performed in Los Angeles?

JC: The show itself got closed down. The cops and the ASPCA were there the whole time and let Stephen Holman and Charles Schneider, the other two acts, do their shows; but when I was supposed to go on, they shut the place down. The cops were looking for me, but weren't very well informed, so they stopped everyone leaving the building who looked weird, asking them if they were Joe Coleman, and I just walked past them.

Anyway, I told a few friends that I'd do the performance at Venice Beach and to meet me there. So then it turned into this trek, where as many people as found out about it through word of mouth drove out to Venice Beach and somehow got organized enough in one spot so that by the time I got there, they were all waiting. I went to this lifeguard station that was about twenty or thirty feet up and had the cars surround it to use their headlights to light it. I did the whole performance on top of this lifeguard station, putting out explosives by diving into the ocean at the end. Fire and water were a real nice combination. It's something that I wouldn't have planned, but happened through circumstance. Another thing was that the police had these helicopters with spotlights circling the theater. It was this great special effect I could never have afforded.

G: There's this attitude in the art world, and even society as a whole, that certain transgressions of law and social order are, if not acceptable, at least pardonable, if they are committed in the name of art. What do you think of today's art?
JC: I don't have much respect for what's termed art today, which seems to do more with fashion and commodities than with personal expression. To me, I have to do what I do and you can call it art, or crime, or abnormal psychology—whatever you want—it's still something I've got to do. The word "art" has been used too easily, to make an investment, or as a game for sophisticated bourgeois people in power. I'm not interested in that, it has nothing to do with what I'm after. I'm doing this stuff for me, not for anybody else. If to justify what I do you have to put labels around it like "art," that's okay for you and society, but I don't care.

G: In terms of that line between what is licensed or licit as art and what is criminal, you've said that if you weren't painting and performing you might well be out there killing people.
JC: I think that potential exists for everyone. People refuse to admit that the killer is inside. Man has this pretense of sophistication and civilization, but he really hasn't changed much since the Cro-Magnon, physically or internally. We're actually more savage because now man has the potential to wipe out the entire planet and has developed far more savage ways to torture his fellow man. He threatens the very host—the planet Earth—that he lives on. Maybe man has always been like

that. Maybe anytime this kind of life develops on a planet, the thing that is man is like a cancer. Man's need to kill is basic and hasn't changed. Men were supposed to kill and hunt for food, and to kill and die to protect the family or the tribe. Now you're not supposed to do that anymore. Now your tribe is no longer this little thing—instead you're supposed to have allegiance to a tribe that is the whole United States. How can you look at it like that? I can only trust what I call my family, the people I let into my life. I can't trust the rest of the world the same way that early man couldn't trust outsiders. I can't trust laws to tell me what to do. I have to decide for myself what's right and wrong. In law it doesn't matter if you're right or wrong, it only matters how good you can bullshit. It has more to do with semantics than morality.

G: Coming from this position of extreme social alienation, it's perhaps your determined stance as this outsider which is what our culture finds so threatening and is unconsciously reacting to in your work.
JC: But it's threatened unnecessarily. How am I really a threat? I'm not killing anybody. Take someone like Richard Speck, a guy whom I believe is trying to communicate pain, but to a point where it's self-destruction. The act of stabbing someone is the most desperate act of communication. It's trying to make a point, trying to connect, trying to reach out and touch someone; but it's a desperate attempt, the one where there's nothing left. If he didn't communicate, he'd be killing himself.

I'm not doing that. I'm coming up with a way to communicate my most horrible rage and frustration. I think everyone felt at some point in their life like they just wanted to explode. Well, what if you could explode and still be there after? What a release that would be. How do you articulate that kind of pain and frustration that would cause someone to go into a McDonald's and start slaying people? I'm not trying to say murder is the right way. I'm trying to point out that there's feelings like that, and those feelings need to be communicated, to be able to be allowed to be expressed. That's where censorship comes into play: if you're not allowed to express those things, then you're going to turn into a Richard Speck.

G: Would you say that your work functions on either that psychiatric construct of catharsis or the more anthropological one of shamanism—some sort of healing force through a shared, ritualistic release of darker, deeper human emotions?
JC: The forces that are at work are the ones that are persona, the ones that motivate me. I can't say that I'm doing this for you or the community, but I don't know if that changes it in this regard. I do it for myself, but in doing so I'm trying to communicate, to connect with other people, and it's up to them to get from it what they can, which in some cases may be cathartic or shamanic in its effects.

G: As much as your work is about communicating this kind of pain, frustration, and alienation, doesn't it become a sort of private self-fulfilling prophesy if the horror, revulsion, and fear you're trying to express are the things that draw a line between you and your work and its audience's instinctive recoil from it?
JC: No, because I can communicate my pain and you can really feel it; you can find those things in yourself. I'm part of this culture, and I'm not so very different from you or anyone else. These same pains that are in me are in you. Whether you have the same life or not really doesn't matter. You're a human being within this particular culture right now. And it seems like this particular culture is full of pain and fear, and all those things that need expression and release.

CHERRY, ME AND CENSORSHIP;

OR, NO FLIES ON ME

Larry Welz

The specter of Censorship hangs over my head all the time, but it never shows its face; not directly to me, anyway; I'm baiting it, trying to get it to come out in the open where we can get a little better look at it. Of course, it doesn't really want to do that. For ten years now, I've been doing this little black-and-white comic book that started out being called *Cherry Poptart* but was later shortened to simply *Cherry*, for reasons I will explain shortly. They were what used to be called "Underground" Comix. Now they don't know what to call them.

Cherry Poptart was conceived as a knock-off parody of Cute

Teenager Comics in general, and a certain more popular line in particular. I made Cherry generic to make her more...uhhh...universal, as well as to cover myself in case I managed to piss somebody off enough to try and sue me: "Any resemblance is purely coincidental, etc...." *Cherry* comics feature lots of hard-core sex. That's part of the setup, which was something like "What if there were a Cute Teenager Comic that showed something more like what teenagers really do...taking lots of drugs, fucking, and doing stupid things?" And what if it was done in the same cutesy, wide-eyed "everything is beautiful" style as the ones you find at 7-11? Cute Girl Who Likes To Fuck.

Another part of the setup: "Underground" or "Alternative" comics at the time (mid-70s) seemed to me to be getting blander and/or disgusting, and when sex came up, it was usually accompanied by dismemberment and/or disembowelment or something even worse. Some of this I'm sure had its place and all that, but I wanted to see something positive about sex, so I wondered how "disgusting" I could make a comic with explicit sex, without it being really disgusting: that is, no violence (well, as little as possible), and not too graphic. Only cute violence (like Disney), no gore, no rape...

"What? No rape? How am I supposed to have this chick get fucked in every single story if she never gets raped?" Don't get me wrong, I'm as aroused by rape scenes as the next guy, but at least I feel guilty about it and rape is not funny. I wanted a funny book. I mean, they're called comics, right?

I didn't feel up to the challenge, so I tried to ignore it for a couple of years. But after a few years, it wouldn't let go, and nobody else was doing it even, so it seemed so obvious to me that something like this was needed. So I hashed it together as best I could and tried to forget about it.

I was greatly inspired at the time by Dan O'Neill, creator of the *Odd Bodkins* newspaper strip which was syndicated by the *San Francisco Chronicle* during the sixties. Dan had assembled the Air Pirates, a group of young, naïve cartoonists from Seattle, and was gunning for Disney. They took the old *Mickey Mouse* characters and did "disgusting" things with them, O'Neill's premise being that these characters aren't even drawn that way anymore, they're now part of American Folklore and therefore in the Public Domain. It was a frontal attack. He wanted Disney to sue him. He wanted the raging bull to charge. When he got his subpoena, he thanked the server effusively. The flames he went down in didn't exactly light up the sky like they were supposed to; but nevertheless, it was a heroic and ballsy act. O'Neill has that penchant for lost causes, and he was just trying to make it work the only way he knows how, which is by being creatively obnoxious.

I decided to apply a slightly different tactic. Rather than a frontal assault, I would dance upon the edges of a precipice, staying just outside the line of what was "socially acceptable," hanging BAs and waving my penis at anybody who might be offended or amused as I go. If anybody reaches out and smacks me down, the sham of "Free Speech" will be exposed for all to see. I'm playing the game of "Nyaah nyaah! Can't catch me!"

Nobody wants to play. But the Phantom Blot of Censorship is out there, and if I can't get them to bite, I want at least to raise his blood pressure a little.

S. Clay Wilson, when he burst onto the scene in the sixties, didn't really open the door as people are fond of saying; he merely showed us that the door was already open. If it's only "line on paper" we can do whatever we want, who gets hurt? And how far can we go? I'm not a pioneer or anything, but I am out here checking for the "edge of the envelope" as they say these days.

Maybe it's something about offense being the best defense, maybe it's just because I want to be censored, and, as we all should know by now, "You can't always get what you want." Not the way you want it anyway. The Phantom Blot is a sneaky guy. He would rather dribble in around your ankles than bite you on the nose while somebody might be looking. Self-censorship is very subtle, like termites. You don't even know they're there until you try to sell your house so you can move somewhere else.

Self-Censorship in *Cherry* Comics

The guy who has been publishing *Cherry* for lo these many years is an old hippie, but he is also a businessman and a survivor. He gets nervous. If I dance too far over that line and the

Phantom Blot decides that it has to kill Cherry, said publisher will be in the line of fire. At least that's what he thinks. I don't want to see him go down; if there's going to be any flames, I want them around me. So I dance along, defiling any sacred taboos I can find within arm's reach.

There are certain things that I don't mess with. The biggest one is Cherry's age. The idea is that she's a teenager, right? But if I depict her as being under eighteen, then she's a child, and it can or could be classified as child pornography, a "bustable offense" in my publisher's words. He wants me to have her be in junior college instead of high school. I take my original line of defense, which is to be generic. It's just a school. Might be a trade school, might be a fucking Vassar. But it makes me wonder...is the act of putting blots of ink on paper that is not even all that white, and that vaguely suggests the image of an underage girl having sex, equivalent to the act of actually abducting an eleven-year-old girl, tying her up in the basement, and forcing her to have sex while you torture her and shoot videos of it? That's a hideous crime, and anyone who does that should be shot in the head immediately. But what about allowing grown men and women even to think about the idea of an underage girl having sex, when nobody gets hurt in the process? Is that legal? We're talking mind control here.

So what I do is just make a big joke of it. I make a big deal about how she's just turned eighteen, she will always have just turned eighteen, as fresh as you can get legally. It's OK for me for now; there are plenty of sacred cows to tip. The other thing is directly assaulting current public figures in too blatant a manner, as I was about to do on the front cover of the book during the Meese Commission hearings. I wasn't really pressured or anything, I was just led to think about it a little. So I changed the one-liner into something really tepid and, yes, generic. I'm glad I did. The gag would have been dated and obscure and not funny by now, and that issue is still in print, as are all thirteen (so far), so I need to be dealing with classical, timeless, immortal themes and larger pieces of history. High-flown talk coming from a Smutmonger. A Phantom Blot dribbles and oozes in around my ankles.

Okay, so what about the shortening of the title? No, I didn't receive any shit from Kellogg's of Battle Creek, Michigan, about the use of the word "Poptart." After I finally did the second issue and it became apparent that we had a seller on our hands, a friend of ours wound up acting as my temporary manager. She was, and probably still is, a hot young bleached blonde megababe who managed head-banger Heavy Metal rock bands. She had so much style she managed to make the spiky black leather torn-up punky-look look cute and sexy. She suggested that we drop the Poptart to avoid the possibility of any such conflict with the Poptart People. I said, well, I doubt if they're going to be a serious threat as long as I don't go into the snack-food business. Then they'll be all over my ass.

But I now begin to notice that the core concept of the thing is going over well enough that the gag of her full name really isn't necessary. "Cherry" by itself actually says it quite nicely, and it's a shorter title that can be blown up larger and be read more easily from a longer distance when it's sitting in the rack in the adult section of the comic-book store. That's it. It wasn't a chickenshit move, it was a design decision, okay? I'm glad I did it, and I think it works.

Part of O'Neill's plan with the *Air Pirates* comics was to have the covers—though they did indeed have some kind of Anarchistic Bad Stuff right there in plain sight—look, at superficial glance, just like a perfectly normal Comics Code Authority-approved wholesome everyday comic book, so that it could be placed surreptitiously on any comic-book rack in any 7-11 or Circle K or whatever, and no one would know the difference. So when some harried housewife with a cranky kid wants a comic book and he's really loud and obnoxious about it so she says "Okay, but I'm gonna pick it out for you, 'cause what do you know? Oh, here's one that looks wholesome—isn't that the Comics Code thingy in the corner there? Sure. Here ya go, kid, take it and shut up!" So the kid's brain ends up getting permanently twisted, and he never trusts authority again. Sort of a psychological letter bomb.

So far, after a full decade, I have received precious little response from the groups, movements, organizations, or Powers that I have been trying to annoy. I did get, through my publisher (in the line of fire, right?) a couple of cranky letters from a staid New England Law Firm representing Archie Comics demanding that we cease and desist and destroy all copies, etc.... That was after the first issue, which contained a story by Larry Todd that directly lampooned the Archie Comics characters in an extremely rude fashion. Copyright infringement blah blah blah...So we took the story out, and stuck something else in there in subsequent reprints, of which there have been many. So now the first ten thousand printed are all collector's items.

Then after #2, they wrote again, noting that we had left out that particular Bad Stuff, but Cherry looks an awful lot like...and her best friend is a dead ringer for...and the cover layout is too similar to our unique design and color scheme so cut it out. Bull's Eye! Tee Hee!

I've gotten no shit at all from feminists of any kind. Actually, it turns out that a whole lot of my fans are women, a goal that I used to dream about but gave up as too hard to do. But Cherry is usually in control of her own destiny, even if she's being silly about it, which was at the time considered an especially Revolutionary Idea. Just a fantasy of mine; what if there was this gorgeous young woman who really loved sex, and didn't have a bunch of hang-ups about it; she just liked to do it? Naaahh... couldn't be. Not where I come from. To my most extreme delight, I have been proven wrong on that one. There are lots of them, and some of them are even cute.

I'm looking for censure, I'm coming on with this chip on my shoulder (although I do wrap it up in a semisarcastic cuteness), and what I get is warm fuzzies from all different kinds of people. I got one letter, well, it wasn't really a letter, it was a small cluster of tiny notes, from a Black guy (I assume he was black, I could be wrong), taking exception to the way I portrayed Black People in my books. The way I portrayed Black People was a parody of the way White People (a lot of them, anyway) still view them. Anyway, this guy cursed me and wanted my dick to shrivel up and fall off into the toilet "Like the piece of shit that it is..." He didn't even want to cut it off himself. That's as close as I've gotten to a Death Threat. I don't get it. Am I that smart, or just lucky? Am I living in a Fool's Paradise, and any minute now they're going to erase my whole existence? Does my warm jovial nature shine through that clearly? Am I that good a dancer? Am I so low and vile in the eyes of Those Whom I Wish to Offend that I am beneath their contempt and not worthy of the merest response or acknowledgment? Hmmm: born an' raised in a briar patch!

At this point I'm just a mouse fart, beneath notice, not anywhere near big enough to be considered dangerous, not worth the trouble it would take to wipe me out. I'm just hangin' out here in the briar patch where nobody wants to go. But it's been ten years now, and *Cherry*'s still alive and kickin'. In fact, she's growing every day, even though she remains "just eighteen." So we'll see. If they find my body on a bathroom floor with a needle in my arm, then you'll know that I was right, they were out to get me. And you're next.

"God, did you hear that? He just compared himself to Lenny Bruce! The nerve of that motherfucker!"

"Really! He doesn't even *do* heroin!"

I remember thinking, as I was dreaming *Cherry* up, that for a comic book to call itself "Underground" it should be dangerous in one way or another. If they even think it's dangerous, then it is. Showing explicit sex as if it was a fun, positive, wholesome, healthy thing could be considered dangerous by some people. I certainly hope so. I wanna be an outlaw. I just don't wanna get out of my chair.

> "I wasn't no backslidin', knee-crawlin', commode-huggin' drunk, I was God's Own Drunk!... And a fearless man!"
>
> —Jimmy Buffett, "God's Own Drunk," from a Lord Buckley routine

Cherry can be purchased from your local comic store. If your store doesn't carry it, it probably doesn't carry *Gauntlet* either. In any case, write to the editor, and we'll steer you to where you can obtain copies.

HOT BOX:
THE WRONG TIME, THE WRONG PLACE
Compiled by Barry Hoffman

The first edition of the English comic, *Hot Box*, was published in 1986. It was to be an independent showcase for the work of recent student graduates, many of whom have since gone on to work for major comic publishers in Britain and the United States.

Editor Martin Salisbury admits that *Hot Box* was not for the fainthearted, but he was, nevertheless, ill-prepared for the intensity of the flak it generated.

In this exclusive interview for *Gauntlet*, Salisbury describes the repressive atmosphere in Britain which led to the extreme reaction *Hot Box* elicited.

G: What inspired the strip dealing with rape in *Hot Box 1*?
MS: The rape strip? It just evolved. Suddenly there it was. Women in Leeds, in the eighties, were suffering the real thing, the threat of danger on the streets; the Yorkshire Ripper was taking his toll—women were being abducted, sexually molested, killed, and mutilated. All women became potential victims, all men potential rapists. No one was safe. Militant women's groups were calling for a curfew to keep men off the streets at night. There was panic, and we were all involved, like it or not.

G: You mentioned that the strip was misinterpreted. In what way?
MS: It was misunderstood! The woman was too sexy, the strip too erotic. One criticism was that she was too well drawn. I did try to balance this by making the men obviously brutal, crude, and almost devoid of individuality. I did try to make them symbolic images in a highly simplified scenario. There was a message, a moral—in rape we all lose, men and women, good and bad, humanity. I thought the strip was rather oversimplified, innocent, and naïve.

Condemnation was pretty universal. My own students recently reported me for owning "hardcore pornography." I've learned to keep a low profile, my attempts at justification seeming to fall on deaf ears. Rape is obviously a completely taboo subject, and not talking about it, not bringing it out into the open, can only make the problem worse.

G: Who attacked this particular strip?
MS: Mostly people I mix and work with at college, "thirtysomething" people. Our review copies of *Hot Box* received very encouraging comments from people in the business, particularly the Society of Strip Illustrators and *Knockabout*. But *International Times,* once a revolutionary organ of freethinking journalism, wasn't enthused. "If the boys who edit this insidious misogyny are reading this, can I just say, keep it from us in the future or we'll put you in touch with a few Leeds women's groups who might be interested to know what you're doing." In light of contemporary events, this was not a threat to be taken lightly.

G: You now feel the inclusion of this strip was a mistake. Why?
MS: As I mentioned, the Yorkshire Ripper was causing dreadful harm at the time, plus there was a break-in at a college gallery by members of a militant women's group who wrecked sculptures they assumed to be pornographic. These are specific incidents, but there was a general atmosphere of sensitivity to anything supposedly "pornographic" at the time. This was Thatcher's Britain, and a determined effort was being made by the government to reestablish Victorian values. I don't consider its inclusion a mistake. In its conception stage, *Hot Box* was established to push the limits of freedom of expression in Comix media. The rape strip did just that.

G: What was the reaction with distributors and comic stores?
MS: Forbidden Planet in London didn't bat an eyelid. They took all we had at the time, with apparently no consequences. Other stores were very offhand about the comic as a whole; we didn't get down to talking about specific strips. It was understandable at some stores, known to be squeaky clean, like Odyssey in Leeds and Manchester, but no others would touch it either...literally. The manager of Timeslip in Newcastle, Northumberland, smiled sympathetically and said, "Don't give up your day jobs." He'd just been raided by the police and said he couldn't afford to take any more risks. The police were only interested in sexually questionable material. Violence didn't seem to bother them.

The worst censorship blow was when we were refused a stall at the Autumn Comic Market in Leeds. We had intended putting on quite a show, with all artists attending, doing signings, and computer monitors displaying animated *Hot Box* adverts.

Conventional distributors gave us short shrift. They were horrified and didn't hide it. I sent a few free review copies to America and Europe, but after the response in Britain, I didn't follow these up. I even began to worry about prosecution by the Customs or the Post Office.

G: In your opening editorial in *Hot Box 2*, you say it is tame in comparison to the first issue. Was this intentional?

MS: It wasn't my intention originally o make it any less a beast than the first issue. It just evolved that way. I was put under some pressure by female friends to temper the drawings of the little girl in "Lady Purple."

G: What has been the impact of the controversy on you personally?

MS: It's been widespread. I have become more resigned to accept other people's bigotry and prejudice. There is a lot of it about. I have gained new insights into civilized society's need to conform, the insidious censorship that goes on all around, and an unpleasant vision of the sterile future we all face if it continues unchallenged. I'm older and wiser and a little disappointed. But life is good! I smoke, I get drunk, I fuck, I eat meat. I draw strange pictures, usually in the privacy of my own home. We've just got to accept that some "do-gooder" is always going to be there, being judgmental, saying, "Stop it! You shouldn't be doing that."

FINDING THE COST OF FREEDOM

Kate Worley

I write a banned comic book.

In fact, if you look at the record of obscenity trials involving comics, I write one of the most universally filthy comic books in the history of the medium. As I look back through the clippings file, several comics appear more than once (*Cherry, Weirdo, Elektra Assassin*), but one appears on almost every bust list since 1986...*Omaha, Omaha, Omaha*.

The sexual content of the book is proportionally small. I didn't realize how small until one zealous New Zealand defending attorney actually counted all of the panels in the first three volumes of *The Collected Omaha,* and found the percentage of sexually explicit material to be about four percent. There is little or no violence, sexual or otherwise. There have been issues with *no* sex in them whatsoever. What's the problem, then? Well, all the sex in *Omaha* is totally explicit, including penile erection and full penetration. We have also included homosexual acts, both male and female. And sex involving more than two persons. Not to mention fully nude dancing. According to some people, this is all made worse by the fact that our characters are funny animals.

I never expected that by writing this little black-and-white, adult, funny-animal soap opera, I would learn about the history of obscenity law throughout the English-speaking world, but it's working out that way. And the cost is about as high as a law-school education. For the comic-book retailer, it's higher.

As I write this, several comic book shops in Toronto are up to their ass in alligators, fighting obscenity charges on a number of titles they carry, including the one I write, *Omaha the Cat Dancer.* The Canadian comic-book retailers have been under fire since 1985's *R.* v. *Wagner,* the court case that inculcated "feminist" principles into obscenity law in Canada. This gave rise to a slew of local cases throughout the country. This is a new and fascinating development in *Omaha's* ongoing obscenity troubles in the Commonwealth countries.

We never got that far before. All the way into the country, wow!

Traditionally, *Omaha*'s difficulties in the Commonwealth countries have begun when the Customs people first opened the boxes. *Omaha* was initially published, as *Bizarre Sex #9,* in September 1981. In October of that year, a shipment of 100 copies was seized by Customs and Excise in England. The case against the importing distributor, Knockabout Comics, was heard in October 1982. Magistrate Audrey Frisby ruled against Knockabout owner Tony Bennett, agreeing with prosecuting solicitor David North that the comic "offended against current standards of propriety" and as such demanded "condemnation" under the 1876 Customs Consolidation Act. As "condemned" books, the comics were destroyed. The cost to Knockabout of these lost books was, Tony Bennett wrote to Dennis Kitchen, "around $700 in various ways (not regretted)."

At the time that letter was written, in October 1982, the police were also holding approximately $20,000 worth of stock for Knockabout, pending hearings.

Cut to May 1990. Kitchen Sink Press publisher Dennis Kitchen receives a letter from Titan Distributors Ltd. of the U.K., explaining apologetically that they will no longer carry *Omaha,* since, with the recent increase of "adult" comic titles, Customs is being extra vigilant in their search and seizure activities, and it makes no sense, economically, to import a book they will never receive because the "Adults Only" label will cause it to be seized. As of this writing, *Omaha* is not being imported into Great Britain.

I don't mean to cast aspersions on Titan, which carried us for many years. They were only dealing with the ugly reality of British Customs. You can see the nature of the Customs problem here: seizure of material, long delay till hearings, economic loss, either through condemnation and subsequent destruction of material, or simply through unavailability for sale of the materials in question. (Anecdotal evidence also suggests that in at least some of the cases, the material is destroyed by Customs before a hearing takes place.)

This pattern is the some throughout the Commonwealth and has, in fact, been repeated with regard to *Omaha* in Canada, Australia, and New Zealand. In most of these reviews, most notably the 1990–91 case in New Zealand, *Omaha* itself has been completely vindicated. Which I'm sure is much comfort to those importers whose seized material has already been destroyed. Okay, so the Brits (and Aussies and Canucks and all) have a set of antiquated laws preventing controversial material from even getting into their countries at the whim of the government (actually, the whim of the individual government official).

Things are better here, right? Here we deal with things at the local level, and the people have an input…"community standards" and so forth. We have a First Amendment which at least permits argument in the courts, and that makes a difference. It is different here, isn't it? No, not very. And when it comes to the impact on the pocketbook, it may be even worse.

The most famous case involving comic books in this country

(thus far), is the case of Friendly Frank. Frank Mangiaracina (now you know why they call him Friendly Frank) is an independent distributor of comic books in the upper Midwest, who also owned several retail comic-book stores. On December 10, 1986, the store in Lansing, Illinois, was entered by six policemen who proceeded to arrest manager Michael Correa on charges of intent to disseminate obscene material. The store was then closed, by authority of the building inspector, on a zoning violation which states that it is a violation to sell adult material within 1,200 feet of a residential area.

While the store managed to reopen a few days later, Michael Correa remained under the charge of intent to disseminate obscene material, a Class A misdemeanor in Illinois. The arrest report, by Officer Anthony Van Gorp, reads as follows: "On November 28, 1986, Officer Zeldenrust and I went to Friendly Frank's Comic Shop... As we looked through the comics, we noticed comic books depicting various sex acts, lesbianism, homosexuality etc..., Officer Zeldenrust and I also observed youths looking through the comics. We also noticed that none of the comics were in a separate viewing area for adults. On December 3, 1986, I went into the shop and purchased $41.10 worth of comics while Sgt. Hoekstra observed my actions from across the street. While I was in the store, I observed a youth looking through a magazine with the words "The adult illustrated fantasy magazine" [presumably *Heavy Metal*—KW} on the cover. The store clerk had made no attempt to stop the youth, who left the store after he noticed I was watching him. The comics were brought to Markham Court and on the advice of the State's Attorney's Office arrest should be made. At 1332 hours (1:32 p.m.) Michael Correa, store manager, was arrested on obscenity charges."

The books found obscene in writing were *Bizarre Sex #5* (featuring *Omaha*), *The Bodyssey, Heavy Metal, Murder* (#2 or #3 or both), *Omaha the Cat Dancer #1–3*, and *Weirdo #17–18*. In later affidavits, some books were added, then dropped, references to "satanically influenced" material were added, then dropped, and references to "youths" reading the material were dropped.

Note also that there was no civilian complaint against the

store. This is true in most of the cases since 1986. With the exception of a recent case in Gainesville, Florida, all the cases I can find documented involving comic books have been initiated solely by law enforcement officers. Most statutes (including the one in Illinois) refer to material "the average person, applying contemporary, adult, community standards" would find as appealing to prurient interest. In practice, however, it appears that the person applying such standards (whatever those are) is the average law enforcement officer.

Michael Correa was found guilty in a finding tendered January 13, 1988. He was fined $750 and put on one year's probation. The judge who presided at the bench trial, Paul T. Foxgrover, warned Correa, telling him that he would be charged much more seriously if he were ever brought up in a similar case. Correa, having been reviled in some local press, including the paper in his hometown of Gary, Indiana, resigned his position as manager of Friendly Frank's, which he had held for two years.

In September of 1989, the Lansing store closed, having lost its lease. Frank sold off the stock cheaply, having nowhere else to put it, selling from 20,000 to 30,000 comics, most of them brand-new (therefore, probably with cover prices between seventy-five cents and two dollars) at ten to fifteen cents each. Using the most conservative figures, Frank lost about $15,000 on the stock.

Michael Correa's conviction was overturned by the First Appellate Court in November 1989.

Frank, through his attorney, Burton Joseph, later brought suit against the city of Lansing for having improperly closed his store in the original arrest. They won, receiving damages of about $15,000, of which some $5,000 went for attorney's fees.

The defense on the obscenity charges had, in total, cost approximately $25,000, for both the original case and the appeal—not, of course, including the loss Frank suffered because of the lost lease. And we're just talking money, here. What price can be put on the loss of Michael Correa's job, his pain and humiliation at being branded a pornographer, and the impact on the public mind of comic books being branded "obscene"?

Of course, it could have been worse.

On November 18, 1987, a Virginia jury decided that Dennis and Barbara Pryba were subject to the forfeiture provisions of the Racketeer Influenced and Corrupt Organizations Act (RICO) for selling merchandise, valued at approximately $105, that had been judged obscene. For this, they forfeited approximately $1 million in businesses, including all stock and personal property in the three bookstores and eight video clubs they owned and operated, nine bank accounts, five vehicles and a warehouse. If they had had a partridge in a pear tree, no doubt it, too, would have been forfeit. And all before sentencing even took place on the obscenity charge, for which both received serious sentences.

This was the first application of the RICO statute in an obscenity prosecution. Most of the assets seized were in no way obscene. In applying the RICO forfeiture, the jury never had an opportunity to consider the legality of the vast majority of the publications and tapes seized. In fact, not all of the materials brought to trial were judged obscene. But that some were was enough to have the Prybas convicted as "racketeers," and thus make all of their assets subject to forfeit.

Defendants of RICO (which was originally targeted at organized crime) will point out that Dennis Pryba was convicted under the federal anti-obscenity statute, making him subject to federal RICO. But twenty-seven states have state RICO laws, as well, which presumably would apply to state statutes (although I don't know this for certain, and have been unable to find current information). RICO apologists might also point out that in congressional hearings on RICO reform, the point was made repeatedly that one instance of violation was not enough for RICO prosecution: for that, a pattern must be shown. What shows a pattern of violation enough to call one a "racketeer" (under the "reforms" of the act, they would now simply be called a "criminal")? *Two* violations.

Frank told me that this is one of the reasons they fought the obscenity charge. If they had accepted one conviction for obscenity, they would have been vulnerable to RICO prosecution if another such charge were levied.

So retailers are at terrible risk if they choose to carry adult material. But is the risk or the reality of economic hardship for the retailer enough reason for the artist to cry "Censorship"? I think so, if the end result of this situation is that an artist cannot get work distributed and sold and, ultimately, must give up doing work having adult themes (at least, sexual themes) in order to eat.

How this hits us personally, with regard to *Omaha,* is easy to document. Even before the local obscenity cases arose, Reed and I felt the economic impact of Omaha's controversial sexual content. Until 1987, Diamond Distribution refused to carry *Omaha* because of its sexual content. Diamond at the time controlled about forty percent of the national distribution of comics. Any comics store which used Diamond as its exclusive distributor could not get *Omaha*. Westfield, the largest comic-subscription service in the country, also refused to carry *Omaha* until 1988. This essentially cut *Omaha* off from people who get their comics by mail. Both of these services, largely because of retailer and consumer pressure, finally changed their minds and began carrying *Omaha*. Another possible reason for their decision was that, during this period, the sexual content of *Omaha* decreased. Not deliberately, simply because the extremely heavy plot got in the way. Whatever the reasoning, it looked as though perhaps, at last, we would have widespread distribution, with consequent increase in royalties and improvement on macaroni-and-cheese dinners.

At the same time, however, retailers looked at the Friendly Frank case...and cringed. Some quit carrying the book altogether. Some put it under the counter, available only on request. Some bagged it, or shrink-wrapped it. None of these strategies are good for business. Sales went up...but not very far.

The busts have gone on. Canada...New Zealand...and, most recently, Florida. As the cases piled up, some retailers who had carried the book, quit. And then our British distributor gave up, which cost us about ten percent of our sales. Back to the mac-and-cheese.

Fortunately, we both like mac-and-cheese. Also fortunately, I was able to get other free-lance work (most notably for Disney's new comic line) that allowed us to continue to pay rent. Otherwise, at least one of us would have had to find a day job. While it is not impossible to produce comics while working a forty-hour week, it is extremely difficult. Comics are highly labor-intensive, especially the way we do them, using the old-fashioned seven-to-nine panel page. A page, counting both my and Reed's time, takes about eight to ten hours of work. An issue of *Omaha* is thirty pages long. With full distribution, including Commonwealth countries, we each can make about as much as a full-time secretary. With restricted distribution, it's Burger Whoopee wages.

So, while the creator is not personally liable in an obscenity case, charges of obscenity *do* affect the creator's ability to make a living. I can understand any creators who therefore choose to censor themselves in order to gain sufficiently wide distribution of their work to get paid decently. And I certainly can understand distributors and retailers being reluctant to carry a work with the history of *Omaha*. They have economic considerations, too, and the consequences of a bust affect them directly, and with infinitely more severity than they do us. But if we knuckle under, the risk is increased for all of us.

Robin Snyder, the editor of *Murder,* put it most elegantly in a commentary in *The Comics Journal*: "When any individual is robbed, cheated, mugged, or is the victim of any force or fraud, he turns to the Law for help, the administration of the Law being one of the functions of Government. But, where does one turn when the mugger is the Law itself?"

Well, at any rate, there is somewhere for comic retailers to turn. Immediately after the Friendly Frank's bust, our publisher, Dennis Kitchen of Kitchen Sink Press, founded the Comic Book Legal Defense Fund, to support the First Amendment fights involving comic retailers. Monies received over and above the costs of Frank's case were put into an interest-bearing account for other fights. But any long battle will need more than the Fund currently has, and the recent Florida cases have seriously depleted it. Retailers are fighting on the front lines for all of us, but they can't do it without support. If you want to help ensure that comics receive their proper protection under the First Amendment, you can send money to: Comic Book Legal Defense Fund, P.O. Box 501, Princeton, WI 54968.

Oh, and if you want to see more of our filthy comics, check your local comics store, or write to Kitchen Sink Press, 2 Swamp Road, Princeton, WI 54968.

THE ART OF HOMOPHOBIA:
DAVID WOJNAROWICZ VS. DONALD WILDMON
Doug Martin

Editor's Note: The following is taken from court transcripts, mailings of the American Family Association, and an exclusive interview with David Wojnarowicz conducted by Doug Martin.

"The representation of my work as it's displayed in the pamphlet distorts very seriously the intention and nature of my work... [It] reduced my work to something that I wouldn't claim as my own and therefore harms my reputation..."

—David Wojnarowicz

"The [Wojnarowicz] lawsuit is an attempt to so something through the courts which the left-wingers have not been able to do in the public arena—shut us up and put us out of business."

—Donald Wildmon
(AFA mailing)

In April 1990, Donald Wildmon's American Family Association (AFA) mailed a pamphlet to all congressmen, religious organizations, and the media, attacking the work of New York artist David Wojnarowicz (labeled by the AFA "a radical homosexual artist/activist with AIDS") as part of an attempt to defeat the reauthorization of the National Endowment for the Arts (NEA).

According to Wojnarowicz, age thirty-five, Wildmon "created a pamphlet with fragments saying these fragments were entire works. What he had done was strip a number of photographs and paintings of all their artistic and political content, take only the sexual images, blow them up and suggest that this was my work."

Wojnarowicz sued the AFA for copyright infringement and $5,000,000 in damages, alleging that the distortion of his work through negative publicity impaired his earning ability as an artist.

On June 26, 1990, U.S. District Judge William C. Conner found for Wojnarowicz, concluding: "The pamphlet could be construed by reasonable persons as misrepresenting the work of the artist, with bringing harm to the artist's reputation and to the value of his works," and prohibited further publication.

In a separate opinion, however, Conner found no malice on the part of the AFA and awarded Wojnarowicz damages of $1. Conner also ordered the AFA to send a notice of clarification to those who received the original mailing.

Wojnarowicz is convinced the judge was duped by Wildmon. "At the trial Wildmon adopted the 'country bumpkin' defense. Here's a guy who's been educated at five universities, who gets up on the stand and says, 'Gee, I don't know the difference between a portrait and a collage.' Those people are very slick and they love claiming ignorance after they assassinate someone's reputation. They're great in terms of using tons of innuendos and half-truths, so they skirt the legal line of libel."

As evidence, Wojnarowicz points out that in the pamphlet Wildmon printed only half of the congressional definition of obscenity. The pamphlet reads: "[Congress prohibited the NEA from funding] depictions of sadomasochism, homo-eroticism, the sexual exploitation of children or individuals engaged in acts of sex..." The AFA left out, Wojnarowicz said, "without scientific, artistic, or social value." Wojnarowicz contends that far from uneducated hicks, the members of the AFA are sophisticated manipulators of their members and the media.

Wildmon, for his part, made the most out of the lawsuit, sending out a fund-raising letter to the AFA's alleged 175,000 members, asking for donations to help build and staff an AFA Legal Team. "I hate to give the ACLU credit," Wildmon wrote, "but the AFA Legal Team will do for Christians what the ACLU has done for pornographers, abortionists, homosexuals, etc."

Wildmon viewed Judge Conner's ruling as a clear victory. In the September 1990 *AFA Journal*, he said, "Our opponents hoped that the lawsuit would put us out of business. Instead it helped make the AFA stronger through building the AFA Legal Team."

Wojnarowicz is in complete agreement on this point. "Wildmon and other religious fanatics," he feels, "are making millions off a painting or photograph I can't sell."

Wojnarowicz, whose work is heavily influenced by his homosexuality, has been diagnosed as having AIDS. An abused child and high-school dropout, he lived on the streets of New York, surviving as a prostitute. It is through his art that he rails against society's inability to come to grips with issues of life and death which he has experienced firsthand.

Unlike the late Robert Mapplethorpe, the notoriety Wojnarowicz has received has not brought fame and prosperity. In court he recounted how NEA chairman John Frohnmayer's response to the AFA pamphlet was that "he finds my work offensive and disgusting and that he would no longer fund works such as mine."

Art critic Philip Yenawine, who testified as an expert witness for Wojnarowicz at his trial, concurred. "...if people have to make a choice between one artist or another...and one of them it looks as if [he] is going to bring them a great deal of censure because people perceive his work to be sexual in nature, then they will decide not to show that work..."

On a personal level, Wojnarowicz has also been scarred. He stated in court: "I live an isolated life. I rarely see people. I spend a great deal of time at home, whether for reasons of health or work and I have come to depend very seriously on my work as the communication I engage in with other people; and I feel this mailing that Wildmon created along with the AFA seriously distorted that communication and caused me a great deal of anxiety and outrage."

For those who feel that any publicity, whether good or bad, is better than no publicity at all, Wojnarowicz is living proof to the contrary. In all probability, he will endure as an obscure footnote in future discussions dealing with the NEA controversy—much as Charles Freeman has been buried under the infamy of 2 Live Crew.

What follows are David Wojnarowicz's views on the NEA, a group he feels is manipulated and misinformed, and his interpretation of his work that the AFA distorted.

G: In your opinion, should there be an NEA?

DW: At this point, I think the NEA would do best to be dismantled if Frohnmayer is going to run it the way he has shown. He has no right to be making the judgments he's making, has no background for it, and has no sensitivity to what images are. And he's perfectly willing to censure [sic], using the tools of his job in terms of vetoes of grants. If the NEA is going to exist with those kinds of restrictions, then I don't think it deserves to exist at all.

G: Besides fundamentalists, you also blame museums and institutions, which determine what is exhibited, for their lack of sensitivity to minorities. Could you elaborate?

DW: The boards of directors of museums make a determination of what culture is for us with their token blacks and their token gays or lesbians. They have one token faggot or one token black to represent what's really an incredible array of culture. As a result, it's no surprise that people are in shock when there's an image of the human body put on exhibition. What we're looking at in museums everyday is culture as it pertains to some rich collectors. The reason why people go into shock when they see an image of the human body is because the institutions aren't doing their jobs in terms of educating people. The idea of the human body as still taboo in 1990 is a total joke.

You see, artists have always created these things, but museums deny their existence by not allowing them to be exhibited. And there will always be a handful of artists who censor themselves, who just want to make money as opposed to dealing with reality or dealing with something political or critical in their work.

G: Do you think the public feels your art is obscene?

DW: A handful of fundamentalist quacks is creating the hysteria. In Illinois I had my retrospective last year, and there were two complaints out of eight thousand people who saw the show. It shows that the public would prefer to look at information. When they see what I present clearly, they don't get hysterical about it. The only people outraged are people who never saw the work. They're the ones writing the letters because someone on the Pat Robertson show tells them to write their congressmen to express their outrage. People who see my work never really find anything wrong with it. People aren't frightened of information. People can handle it.

ON OUR BACKS
GETS KICKED IN THE ASS
Compiled by Barry Hoffman

On *Our Backs* is a magazine that, according to former editor Marcy Scheiner, "publishes depictions of explicit lesbian sexuality." You won't find it at major chains because of its sexual explicitness, and Scheiner says some women's bookstores refuse to stock it because they feel it is anti-feminist.

On Our Backs' worst brush with censorship, however, came when the magazine decided to go glossy. Its San Francisco printer did not have the capability at the time, so the editors shopped in the Midwest (where prices are best). Actually, they were solicited by Dimension Graphics, a printer in Kansas. The magazine went with Dimension Graphics, says Scheiner, "because they'd shown a lack of homophobia by printing explicit heterosexual porn." To be on the safe side, however, the magazine's art director "grilled the sales rep about what they would and would not print and was assured that even penetration would not be a problem."

The first issue went smoothly. With the next issue, the honeymoon ended.

With all material at the printers, *On Our Backs* received a call from Dimension Graphics that two photos in a pictorial of Aminta had crossed the line. Scheiner considers the spread to be "the most soft-core pictorial in the issue. She was playing with a dildo for God's sake! But it was a black dildo."

The concern was not only a possible delay in publication, but the very real possibility that the printer might destroy original material. The entire contents of the magazine—original photos, editorial copy, ads—was in the hands of a bunch of unknown white heterosexual men in Kansas. "For all we knew, if we didn't cooperate with them we might never see any of it again—a major loss for us as well as for our contributors," Scheiner relates.

The staff relented and sent new material to replace what had offended the printer. But Dimensions Graphics wasn't through. A week later the printers called *On Our Backs,* this time objecting to Annie Sprinkle's photos of a woman licking pussy through Saran Wrap. According to Scheiner, "These photos are not only hot, but they are essential educational tools. They represent a very rare phenomenon: graphic portrayals of how lesbians can protect themselves from sexually transmitted diseases." These, too, were replaced.

With the magazine finally printed and shipped, Scheiner confronted Dimension Graphics to determine whether the offending art violated Kansas law or just the printer's sensibilities. She relates her conversation: "I phoned the printer and inquired as to which laws I should be aware of in planning future issues of *On Our Backs.* He ran a rap about penetration, explicit or implied. 'Yes,' I said, 'we understand, but exactly which law does this fall under?' He unabashedly informed me that his policy had nothing to do with the law, that it was a 'corporate decision. This is where we draw the line. These are our personal mores.'"

Arguably, while printers can reject any material they find objectionable (there are no laws to protect the client even *after* contracts have been signed), the abuse of power by the printer here was particularly insidious. Scheiner feels: "By actively soliciting business from publishers of sexual materials, then asking them to tone down their work, Dimension Graphics is employing tactics alarmingly similar to those used by the anti-abortion movement, who pose as 'abortion counselors' and then show vulnerable pregnant women grisly films of aborted fetuses."

SAN FRANCISCO V. *BASIC INSTINCT*

Rebecka Wright

In April and May 1991, San Francisco played hostess to Hollywood. Hollywood demonstrated that it clearly has a lot to learn about sensitivity, among other things. San Francisco just...demonstrated.

The occasion was the filming of *Basic Instinct*, a big-budget sex thriller of the gruesome variety that is so common these days: one or more homicidal maniacs are pursued by a brutal cop, who is supposed to be the good guy. Along the way, the landscape is strewn with pretty corpses. In this case, the cop is played by Michael Douglas, whom you may remember as the victimized adulterer of *Fatal Attraction*. He is directed by Paul Verhoeven, the Dutch intellectual who is known here in the United States for such pieces of subtle artistry as *Robocop* and *Total Recall.* The story is from a $3 million screenplay by Joe Eszterhas, late of *Rolling Stone* magazine, and writer of *Betrayed* and *Jagged Edge.* The corpses are played by various, as always.

The local filmmaking community was happy to have some work in town, less happy that the work itself was such typical trash. It seems that the SF Film Commission is badly understaffed, and the film-selection process is not terribly receptive to outside input. Productions that get the green light are normally productions with large budgets, so that the city can rake in some healthy revenues, and are not often of the socially relevant type that would delight the people who live here in liberal 'Frisco. *Basic Instinct*, as the title itself suggests, is about as far from elevated consciousness as it gets. One local industry worker mused, "It's peculiar that they choose such sensational and violent films for this beautiful city."

At first, it appeared to be just dreary business as usual. Things heated up real fast though, when the Gay and Lesbian Alliance Against Defamation (GLAAD), a national media-watchdog organization, obtained a copy of the script. This particular film features three women, all of them clearly depicted as either lesbian or bisexual. This wouldn't have been a problem, really, except that all three are also depicted as murderers and at least one as a psychopath. While distasteful and statistically unlikely, to put it mildly, even this could have been tolerated, if it weren't for the fact that gay men and particularly lesbians are portrayed, almost without exception, in just such mentally unbalanced and/or criminal ways every time they appear on the U.S. silver screen. The transvestite psycho-killer (who actually may or may not be gay) in *Silence of the Lambs* was cited as a recent example of this trend. Deciding that enough was enough, GLAAD and Queer Nation protested when filming began at a local gay bar, the Rawhide II.

In part, the demonstrators felt that the movie was inflammatory and would exacerbate the problem of anti-gay violence. While this point is arguable, it was clear that to film it here in San Francisco would be ridiculously insensitive. San Francisco is supposed to be a sanctuary of sorts for gay and lesbian people, though gay bashing happens here, too. To film the movie in an actual gay community establishment—the Rawhide II—really added insult to injury.

The Rawhide II is owned by Ray Chalker, the publisher of a local gay weekly newspaper, the *San Francisco Sentinel.* There is little love lost between the more politically active members of the gay community and Mr. Chalker, who has a habit of supporting conservative causes, most recently the election of Republican Pete Wilson to the governorship of California. (Governor Wilson recently vetoed AB101, a bill that would have outlawed job discrimination based on sexual orientation.) Mr. Chalker says that the filmmakers assured him that the film was not homophobic (or lesbophobic, as it came to be called), and he believed them, although he had not read the script himself. His cooperation with the makers of *Basic Instinct* lead some in the community to accuse him of profiteering and even treason.

Things started to get ugly. The Rawhide II, neighboring businesses, the *Sentinel* offices, and the Castro district were vandalized, most notably with "Kill Ray" graffiti. Mr. Chalker reported that he was getting death threats on his answering machine. Queer Nation denied any involvement with any of these activities, and concentrated on organizing an advertising boycott of the *Sentinel.* There were rumors bandied about that Mr. Chalker was making up the death-threat stories in an attempt to regain the sympathies of the community. This possibility seems only slightly more plausible than three rampaging lesbian psycho-killers. Answering machines aside, it's hard to argue with spray paint. The filming moved from the Rawhide II to various other locations around the city, some of which were vandalized, all of which were subject to protests.

The demonstrations were modeled after the successful ACT UP protest of a 1989 episode of NBC's *Midnight Caller*, which was inspired by Randy Shilts' book *And the Band Played On.* ACT UP was able to shut down production by making so much noise at an outdoor set that it was impossible to film. Filming resumed the next day, but the producers realized that they couldn't afford to shoot in the city if the demonstrators couldn't be mollified. Since the program was very definitely based in San Francisco, moving out of town was considered the course of last resort. They invited the input of the community for a follow-up episode which ran the next season. GLAAD and Queer Nation weren't able to generate the decibel level that would have been needed to shut down *Basic Instinct,* but they were a constant irritant. The resulting publicity generated closer scrutiny by city officials, who were so outraged that they made public statements outlining just how outraged they were.

Finally the *Basic Instinct* filmmakers agreed to sit down and listen to the protesters' concerns. To the surprise of everyone, including director Verhoeven, screenwriter Eszterhas has ended up being sympathetic to the protesters' objections.

Mr. Eszterhas had previously described his script as "organically constructed," implying that to change anything would compromise the whole. He also argued that "if we've reached the point where any minority refuses to accept the possibility of a psychotic or murderer among them, then we've reached the state where the only villains can be male WASPs." (In all fairness, the villain in Mr. Eszterhas's *Betrayed* was a male white supremacist, and a previous film by Mr. Verhoeven, *The Fourth Man*, had received kudos from the gay community for its sensitive portrayal of a gay man.) Mr. Eszterhas suggested some changes to the script, which the protesters said were an improvement, although they didn't really change the homophobic character of the film. In any case, the changes were rejected by Mr. Verhoeven. The production company, Carolco Pictures, issued a statement accusing the demonstrators of "censorship by street action."

Carolco got a court order to keep the protesters 100 feet from the filming locations, and banning loud noises, the offensive use of flashlights, and glitter. Yes, *glitter.* (It's those little touches that make me love San Francisco.) The protesters kept showing up. Some were arrested. One or two were roughed up by a rogue crew member. Filming wrapped up here and moved on to the next location, as scheduled.

The protesters felt that a victory had been achieved, although no real substantive changes occurred, because the issue of Hollywood homophobia was pushed out of the closet for the first time in years. Many hoped that the issue would continue to be raised. According to a Queer Nation press release: "We will not let up until the censorship of our lives ends, and we finally see our richness and complexity as a community reflected back to us on the silver screen."

Are Protests Censorship?

Civil disobedience in this country goes all the way back to the Boston Tea Party. Respect for private property has not figured prominently in our history. Naturally, this troubles business interests, and movie companies are definitely businesses. They are also the creators of a popular art form. While I believe that business is a valid target of protest, the nature of the media business limits the forms of protest which can be properly used against it. To be effective, the protest must be able to generate heat, but hopefully this can be accomplished without extinguishing free speech. Likewise, it is important for both the protesters and the target of protest to realize that violence against property or ideas does not justify violence against human beings. Some people characterized the demonstrations as attempts to shut down the movie entirely. The protesters denied that this was their intention. In combing the records, I have to agree that the goal of the protesters seemed to be dialogue, not censorship. However, some of the tactics that were used teetered dangerously close to interference with the free speech of the filmmakers. Attempting to shut down production literally means to shut up the producers. Though the possibility of success seems remote, it does happen. ACT UP successfully—if temporarily—shut down filming on *Midnight Caller.* ACT UP also succeeded in shouting down U.S. Secretary of Health and Human Services Louis Sullivan at a San Francisco–based international AIDS conference in 1990. Governor Wilson was recently drowned out at a Stanford University function, after he vetoed AB101. Of course, government officials will always have another chance to speak—if not to the same audience—but the people who wouldn't let them talk have lost the moral high ground. Ultimately, it is better to let them have their say. It is possible to learn something, if only where the weakness in their argument lies.

Perhaps some people should not be heard because they are racist, sexist, homophobic, fascist, or part of a corrupt and even murderous government. These people are dangerous influences. They are bad people. Really bad people. The distillation of this argument is that really bad people do not have the right to be heard. The problem is that this can go both ways. There are plenty of people who would love to deny the right of free speech to pervert homosexuals, godless atheists, morally bankrupt pornographers, disgusting miscegenationists, murdering abortionists, *and* fellow travelers because, in their view, these are really bad people. Dangerous influences, if you will.

So if we all agree that bad people should not be allowed to speak, how do we decide who defines what makes a "bad person"?

I'm not willing to give *anyone* the power to decide such a question. I'm too afraid the perverts might come out on the losing end. This is not paranoia on my part. There are many examples in recent history of "dangerous" people being denied their rights by the U.S. government. Japanese-Americans were herded into detention centers during World War II, ostensibly because they were a threat to the war effort. Communists were subjected to social and professional ostracism during the Cold War, because of their "dangerous" ideas. Most recently, the War on Drugs has enabled the government to severely restrict civil rights, under the cover of protecting the citizenry from a powerful and dangerous enemy. None of these incidents has inspired an enormous outcry from the people of the United States, demanding that *all* citizens retain their constitutional rights.

For every ACT UP leader, there is someone like the Reverend Donald E. Wildmon. In the case of the *Midnight Caller* protest, ACT UP did not approve of the way a bisexual person with AIDS was portrayed. Wildmon and his American Family Association did not approve of the way a homosexual couple was depicted on *thirtysomething,* and so instituted one of their famous write-in campaigns. These groups are on opposite ends of the political spectrum, but they used very similar tactics to achieve their goals. Both attempted to hit the network in the pocketbook. The main difference is that ACT UP attempted to *prevent* the filming of the episode, by making production too expensive, while Wildmon threatened sponsors with boycotts *after* the episode had already aired.

ACT UP believes that its actions are justified because the very lives of People with AIDS (PWAs) are at stake. There is indeed a state of emergency surrounding the AIDS crisis. (A similar argument could be used by anti-abortion activists, but that's another article.) However, emergencies have often been misused as an excuse to suspend the rights of others: just ask an elderly Japanese-American or a former 30s-style Communist. Hindsight has shown that these people were probably not real threats, and neither was *Midnight Caller*. TV shows don't kill PWAs, AIDS kills PWAs.

The protests of *Basic Instinct* were well conceived and succeeded in opening the lines of communication between the filmmakers and the protesters, without overly interfering with free speech on either side. Apparently, at least one mind was changed, though it remains to be seen whether Mr. Eszterhas will ever write a screenplay populated with happy, healthy lesbians. However, the scapegoating of Mr. Chalker was irritating. The vilifying charges of profiteering and treason were thrown around in an irresponsible manner. It is not necessarily treason to disagree with the tactics of your fellows. Mr. Chalker is an active member of the gay community, even though his politics may be objectionable to many. When the protesters began characterizing him as a traitor, the lunatic fringe came out and threatened death to the infidel. Even though they deny responsibility for these threats, the protesters *must* accept blame for starting the finger pointing. By casting about for someone nearby to pin the blame on, they set up Mr. Chalker for the nastiness to come. I certainly hope that none of the protesters ever has a lapse of judgment like Mr. Chalker's, or they, too, may feel the wrath of anonymous terrorists.

There are director/auteurs, especially in Europe, who will put nonstereotypical homosexual characters into their films—people like Woody Allen *(Manhattan)*, Blake Edwards *(Victor/Victoria)*, Paul Bartel *(Scenes of the Class Struggle in*

Beverly Hills), and Pedro Almodovar (*Labyrinth of Passion, Law of Desire*). Few of these are considered "Hollywood" directors. While the protesters are right and their complaints are valid, they are sadly mistaken if they think that Hollywood acceptance is worth gaining.

Hollywood movies do not reflect complexity or reality. They never have. That's not what they are for. They are propaganda for the status quo. They can inspire mindless patriotism, supply dreams for people who haven't got enough imagination to dream their own dreams. They can make people think that everything is under control and will turn out okay in the end, even as society crumbles outside the theater. I don't think that they have the power to change a bigot's mind, but there isn't any harm in trying, as long as we don't confuse success in the media with success in any other realm of existence. To paraphrase Urvashi Vaid, who wrote about outing in a previous issue of *Gauntlet,* bad characterizations in the movies are not the cause of homophobia—they are merely its exhibits.

People thought that improved media images would improve the lot of African-Americans. This is not the case for the majority of American blacks today. Sure, there are a few more acting jobs available. But more and more young blacks die by violence. Poverty is heavily concentrated in the black community. Perhaps all those positive images in the past three decades were used as a smoke screen to make people think that some substantive advancements were being made, when the reality was very different. Perhaps these images even acted as a tranquilizer that kept those whose lives were not improving from demanding to know why.

This is not the end I would like to see for the Gay Power movement. I'd like to see some changes happen that really mean something—the repeal of sodomy laws, for instance. A Hollywood confection like *Three Dykes and a Baby* somehow doesn't impress me as a real social gain. Mainstream movies are for the mainstream. It's silly to depend on them for validation. There is no reason why the gay community should need to beg for crumbs of acceptance from a boring, corporate Hollywood.

It certainly hasn't worked for Chicanos, Asian-Americans, or even, after all this time, women. All of these groups are still better served by independent productions than by grandiose blockbusters.

That's why it's so great that there are gay and lesbian film festivals springing up all over the country. Every year scores of new films from within the community are exhibited.

These are proof positive that homosexuals the world over can speak for themselves, can make their own entertainment, and *can* see themselves reflected off of the silver screen, in all their richness and complexity. Sometimes a few gems leak out into the big, bad world out there. There are many artists within the community who deserve our support. People like Jennie Livingstone, director of *Paris Is Burning;* Rob Epstein, director of *The Life and Times of Harvey Milk;* Marlon Riggs, director of *Tongues Untied;* Harvey Fierstein, writer/star of *Torch Song Trilogy;* Donna Deitch, director of *Desert Hearts;* Micki Dickoff, director of *Our Sons,* a recent ABC movie; and many, many others. The power lies in seizing the means of production. Then you can always say what you wish rather than beg someone else to say it for you.

STILL LURKING IN THE SHADOWS, AFTER ALL THESE YEARS

Michael C. Botkin

National Geographic, that stalwart bastion of mainstream blandness, recently published an article about West Hollywood. I was curious as to how they would deal with the fact that the township is a majority Queer community, and indeed, this was a major factor in its secession from the city of Los Angeles. What would the mainstreamers make of the colorful natives on their little safari to this urban jungle?

They did what most of the press does with the Queer issue: ignored it as much as possible, and wildly distorted the little they did perceive.

There was one mention of the gay community in the several thousand words of the text, and this was a brief reference to the Gay and Lesbian Community Center. However, the mention came only in the context of a more prolonged discussion of a heterosexual woman with AIDS who received services from the center. The more than ninety-eight percent of the center's clients who are gay and lesbian remained invisible.

On a graphic level, there were two photos of gay men. The first was a teenage junkie hustler working the streets, the second a horribly emaciated Person With AIDS clearly on his deathbed. This pretty much sums up the conservative stereotype of gays: Outlandish Degenerates and/or Dead Meat Specials. *NG* was striking a "compassionate" pose, along the lines of "Isn't it a shame that homosexuals are doomed to brief and miserable lives of quiet desperation cut short by an early and painful death." The more hard-core right-wingers take a harsher tack, cruising Gay Pride festivals and selectively targeting the most outlandish leather queens and motorcycle dykes they can find for portrayal in videos designed to support crusades against gay rights.

The liberal wing of the media offers a far less pejorative view of the queer community, but ultimately it is almost as skewed and distorted. *The New York Times,* which for years refused to use the word "gay," insisting upon the clinical term "homosexual," recently began providing extensive coverage of gay and lesbian issues. Currently, scarcely a week goes by without its publishing a major article on Queers, whether it's the latest purge of gays from the military, our presence at the Democratic National Convention, or a lawsuit against the Boy Scouts of America for homophobic discrimination.

But this awareness extends only to the most yuppified aspects of the Queer community. It's as though they can recognize only those of us who most closely resemble their own image of the Ideal Citizen: exemplary soldiers, delegates to presidential conventions, perfect Eagle Scouts.

This is particularly noticeable in the *Times*'s almost obsessive attention to "the gay market." Announcing that major mainstream advertisers have finally decided that the gay market is "too big to ignore," it has printed several articles on the prospects of "the Gay Slicks," glossy magazines targeted at moderate upscale "gaystream" audiences. In today's tight advertising markets, the prospect of wealthy, high-living Guppies (from "Gay Urban Professionals") just waiting to buy name-brand vodka, expensive household toys, and costly vacations is simply too alluring to resist.

This is not to say that the Queer community doesn't have its fair share of junkie hustlers, terminal PWAs, leather queens, bike-dykes, and well-heeled gaystreamers with high discretionary incomes. It's just that these easily recognizable subgroups are clearly, to anyone at all familiar with the community, just the tip of the iceberg. And, as far as I can tell, the mainstream media are totally unaware of this. In all fairness, I don't think that most editors have a fixed homophobic policy. But they see what they expect to see, and anything that goes counter to their expectations so confuses them that they simply ignore it. This confusion was apparent in local newspapers' recent bewildered attempts to cover the rise of the Queer National Movement. Like ACT UP, its role model, Queer Nation began in New York City (in 1989) and spread quickly to the other gay urban meccas, like San Francisco and Los Angeles. Queer nationals favor in-your-face demonstrations, civil disobedience, bizarre acronyms (my personal favorite: DORIS SQUASH for "Defending Our Rights in the Streets, Super Queers United Against Savage Heterocentrism," an anti-queer-bashing group) and an ultra-democratic openness based on consensus process. Finding the AIDS focus of ACT UP too restrictive, local QN chapters sponsored a multitude of aggressive consciousness-raising events, like Queer "outings" to suburban malls, demonstrations at fundamentalist churches, and protests of homophobic movies like *Basic Instinct*.

The media just don't know what to make of us. They weren't sure if the obscure acronyms were serious or not (mostly not), and they couldn't see if or how we were different from ACT UP. A writer for one of the local dailies followed a crowd of Queer Nationals around during the rather spirited protests during the invasion of Iraq; in his column he called them "ACT UP types" (which actually wasn't a bad description). But he was dinged for misattribution and had to admit that he really didn't know who they were or what group they actually "represented."

The absurdly decentralized structure of Queer Nation/San Francisco drove local journalists up the wall. They would attribute a demonstration to QN, only to be huffily informed that it had been sponsored by this or that "focus group," imprecisely affiliated with QN but *not* endorsed by the parent organization. After about eighteen months of frenzied and troubled existence, QN/SF folded last year, but only after having sparked a plethora of now-freestanding committees and activist grouplets. To me, it's obvious that all these fragments are distinctively Queer National in their goals, membership, and heritage, but to the mainstreamers they are just a swamp of random acronyms.

Back in 1989 it had been so easy! There was just one, single Queer activist group. If any queer militants in black leather jackets showed up disruptively someplace, you could simply call them "ACT UP" and you knew you'd be right. But ACT UP/Golden Gate split from the parent ACT UP/SF, in 1990, and QN was formed soon thereafter (no need to go into the details of the split, as it was totally arcane to the mainstreamers). Then, to top it all off, QN implodes and splinters into a dozen fragments, which scatter across the political horizon like cue balls.

To them, this new movement was an impenetrable maze, and their instinctive response was, therefore, to ignore it as much as possible. When Queer Nationals trashed San Francisco Chief of Police Frank Jordan during a riot, ripping off one of his shoes, many attributed this anarchistic militance to (of all people!) the Revolutionary Communist Party, a group that scarcely exists anymore and has not, for some time now, dared to show its red flags in the Queer Castro district, where the Jordan melee took place.

(Since Jordan became mayor of San Francisco shortly afterward, our community deemed it advisable to play down the whole incident as much as possible and didn't particularly challenge the misattribution. The shoe itself was ritually immolated, mounted upon a donut box).

Likewise, the above-mentioned protests of the Iraqi war, and, more recently, demonstrations against the Rodney King verdict were heavily Queer events in San Francisco, a detail the media largely ignored (or, to be fair, perhaps just didn't notice). Of course, there is a certain advantage to this lack of basic knowledge: it impeded mainstream intervention and counter-action. As Mark Pritchard, editor of *Frighten the Horses,* puts it: "For now I take comfort in the momentary inattention of the law enforcement/intelligence community: 90s groups like Queer Nation can bloom overnight, scandalize the squares for a year, then blow apart like dandelions before the Feds even notice."

Tactical considerations aside, it is clear that the overall affect of Queer Invisibility is to keep more gays and lesbians in the closet and disempower the Queer community as a whole.

Few groups in the United States have as little control over how they are portrayed in the mainstream media as we do. While racist and sexist commentary is discouraged, or at least allowed rebuttal (on the rather frequent occasions when it happens anyway), talk-show hosts can openly fag-bash away for hours, and Hollywood can grind out endless empty thrillers based on psycho-killer Queers without fear of any serious reprimand. If we suggest that these attacks entitle us to equal time to respond, their jaws drop in amazement. If we protest so effectively that we can't be ignored—as we did around *Basic Instinct*—they declare us "terrorists."

I see two factors on the horizon that are likely to alter Queer's currently shadowy status. The first is the growing militance of the Queer community, which is already hypersensitive to our portrayal in the media. A major national gay group is GLAAD, Gay and Lesbian Alliance Against Defamation, with numerous local chapters and a policy of aggressively monitoring media coverage of Queer issues. Combined with Queer National zaps against the worst of the homophobes, and the contrasting lure of the lucrative Guppie market, this influence is likely to tilt the balance of power in media representation debates in favor of the Queers and against the reactionaries and fundamentalists, who until now have succeeded in cowing advertisers with (probably empty) boycott threats.

The second is the emergence of openly gay and lesbian journalists in the mainstream media (e.g. the National Association of Gay and Lesbian Journalists). These closeted workers have been there for decades, of course, but only recently have they begun to feel entitled to representation and input into editorial policy. Ironically, although they have clearly benefited from the new Queer militant wave, they are, as a group, fairly hostile to it. Now they have begun to organize, to "come out" on the job, and to agitate for better mainstream coverage of Queer Issues. It was the influence of just such a group at *The New York Times* which inspired their newly awakened interest in such things as the Gay Market. When the militant wing develops enough clout to require mainstream change, the newly out mainstream journalism Queers will be ready to step in and provide it. It will doubtless still be skewed, but Goddess, it's got to be better than what we've got now.

HATE AND THE ART OF QUEER MEDIA SPINS

Andy Mangels

In 1988, I was involved in a protest against *The Oregonian*, the largest newspaper in the state of (where else) Oregon. Sponsored by Queers United Against Closets (QUAC), Portland's early version of ACT UP, we were distressed with the gay-bashing editorials by editor David Reinhart. He blamed the AIDS crisis on the gay community and refused to cover anything positive relating to the gay community. We staged a "die-in" on sheets of butcher paper, tracing outlines of our bodies and writing in the names of deceased Oregonians who had died of AIDS.

The butcher-paper roll was delivered to Reinhart's office

door, and our demonstration ended. One TV station hurriedly covered the event, and even *The Oregonian* had a small piece on it. Staffers later told people that Reinhart had cried when he saw the butcher paper roll representing the lives lost.

That was an election year, and the gay community of Oregon already faced a bitter battle. The government had passed a bill which protected state employees from job discrimination due to sexual orientation. A small conservative group called Oregon Citizens' Alliance began a petition drive to overturn the bill, succeeding in getting a confusingly worded measure on the ballot.

The OCA misdirected the public with a commercial showing a fearful child about to be adopted by two male lovers, obvious "child-molester" caricatures. They claimed that the governor's bill allowed such evil to corrupt children. While TV stations pulled the ad, little play was given in the media as a whole to the struggle into which the gay community was entering.

Despite last-minute newspaper nonendorsements of the OCA's Measure 8, the outlying country areas of Oregon pushed the ballot box to the brink of bigotry. The measure no one thought would win became a cold reality. Last year the OCA sniffed the winds again and felt the time was right to make its grand play. The OCA introduced to the public a petition that declared illegal "perverse and unnatural" homosexuality, sadism, masochism, pedophilia, and necrophilia (these last two already illegal). The wording of the measure would ban government promotion or protection of any of these, and require schools to teach that these life-styles were wrong.

This time, not only did Oregonians themselves wake up to the threat of the bigoted fringe, but so did *The Oregonian* itself, along with the rest of the media. As OCA cronies went signature gathering in the malls, positive news pieces about the gay community began popping up weekly, then several times a week. When several store chains and shopping malls went to court to keep the OCA from petitioning on their doorsteps, the reporters crowded in to flaunt the hoped-for failures of the right-wing bigots. When a poster appeared around the state declaring: "Free Jeffrey Dahmer, All He Did Was Kill Homosexuals," and listing the OCA's address, the cause became a national phenomenon.

The TV magazine show, *20/20,* shot an unflattering portrait of the OCA and its leaders, comparing them to the Ku Klux Klan and labeling them a "hate group." The segment helped strengthen both sides, however; while it gave the gay community new supporters, it also gave the OCA a new infusion of interest and money from bigots around the country.

Meanwhile, the OCA's video of San Francisco Gay Pride antics, which were meant to shock the public, didn't find the support it had hoped for. *The Oregonian* and other state newspapers became targets of the OCA-sponsored boycotts due to their editorial policies. These were called off after meetings with the OCA; yet, if anything, the gay coverage became stronger and more visible than ever before.

The OCA attempted citywide measures of the same sort as their statewide initiative, in Portland, Corvallis, and Springfield. When the Portland signatures were turned in, a large percentage was disqualified, and the measure did not qualify for the ballot. Corvallis, a college town, defeated the measure handsomely. Springfield didn't. Immediately upon passage, the OCA was calling for the removal of "pro-gay" books from the town library.

On July 3, the day before Independence Day, the OCA turned in their state-wide signatures, far in excess of the required amount. Many civil rights activists spent a non-celebratory weekend. The signatures were counted and recounted, but the devils had done their deeds. The "No-Special-Rights Initiative" soon became Measure 9.

What will Measure 9 accomplish if it passes in November? All books, encyclopedias, and recordings which do not label homosexuality "perverse and unnatural" will be removed from public and school libraries. All schoolteachers and any state workers who deal with children will be grilled about their sexuality; if found to be—or suspected of being—homosexual, they will be removed from any access to children. The state of Oregon will be forced to abolish any kind of anti-discrimination laws regarding housing, employment, medical aid, etc.

Not chilling enough? All hate-crimes laws will be removed from books as well, removing gay bashing as a crime. Business and liquor licenses, all state controlled, will be pulled and/or denied to any business thought to cater to gay clientele. Public television and radio, if it is receiving any government money, will be forced to air anti-gay propaganda. All state-funded AIDS agencies will also be forced to espouse anti-gay rhetoric or be shut down.

Constitution be damned, the OCA is fighting faggots here!

Into this vicious climate of hate, the civil rights activists have finally seen the media stepping in to represent them. *The Oregonian* now has daily articles on gay themes, and every movement of the pro-OCA or anti-OCA forces is tracked carefully. Electronic media are not far behind. Marchers in this year's Gay Pride Parade noted humorously that for perhaps the first time in national history, the media estimated the same number of marchers and participants as the Pride committee itself!

The media is having an easy time presenting a case against the OCA. The hate group has split recently from the Republican party, which denounced them. The Oregon Medical Association gave the OCA's message a bad diagnosis, and coalitions of churches are preaching anti-hate and anti-OCA messages from the pulpit. Even the Oregon Council of Architects recently changed their name to Council of Oregon Architects due to the embarrassment over their monogram.

With storm clouds rending the horizon, some gay leaders are thanking the OCA for bringing civil-rights solidarity to the state, yet such thanks are premature. Still, a victory has been won in the media. Four years ago, a roll of butcher paper with traced bodies of death gained tears. Today a measure which threatens to split a state and destroy civil rights has gained much more attention to the plight of the beleaguered gay community.

Ironically, the politics of hate have impassioned the media far more than the politics of loss.

THE MISSING DEMAND IN THE GAY AGENDA

Michael Medved

In all the nearly six hours of speeches at the recent gay and lesbian march on Washington, and in all the countless manifestos generally associated with today's powerful push for homosexual rights, there is one demand, one agenda item, that has been conspicuous by its absence.

To the best of my knowledge, no significant leader of this movement has suggested that we implement "affirmative action" for homosexuals.

It seems fair to ask why not.

The drive for gay rights is repeatedly compared to previous civil rights campaigns for African-Americans, Latinos, women, and others. All of those previous movements, however, have called for affirmative action—or, on occasion, outright quotas—as a key precondition for progress.

With gays currently portrayed as American's latest disadvantaged minority, why shouldn't the same strategy be applied to them?

The two-part answer to this question demonstrates why it is so terribly misleading to describe the movement for gay rights as just one more campaign for equal justice.

The first obstacle in establishing any quota program for gays and lesbians is that this segment of the population is so notoriously hard to count. The controversy concerning recent studies that show homosexuals as one percent of American adults, rather than the ten percent that gay activists claim, only highlights the difficulties in reaching a consensus on accurate numbers.

The problems in this process would be enough to drive any bureaucratic bean counter around the bend. What percentage of a given profession would have to be openly homosexual before that elite could satisfy authorities that gay people had been granted equality of opportunity? Who would qualify as "gay" anyway? What about a suburban father and husband who had a brief homosexual affair five years ago? Could you count him as gay for affirmative action purposes?

But beyond the obvious problems in enumerating who is gay and who is not for the purposes of governmental scorekeeping, there is another powerful reason that homosexual activists aren't interested in establishing some quota system based on sexual orientation.

In many crucial areas traditionally targeted by affirmative-action programs, gays are already overrepresented—and they know it.

In fact, one of the major themes that emerged in the Washington march (which I attended as a spectator) involved an unmistakable note of gay triumphalism—unabashed pride in the many positions of influence and authority now occupied by homosexuals.

Andrew Kopkind, for instance, in his much-discussed article "The Gay Moment" in *The Nation* declared:

> There would hardly be modern art, literature, or philosophy without gay sensibility.... Broadway is bursting with gay plays, big book awards go to gay authors.... "Queer theory"—also known as lesbian and gay studies—is explored by scholars and students at hundreds of colleges... There are hundreds of new organizations formed by gays in professions (journalism, law, medicine, psychotherapy, teaching).... The ascension of gay people to positions of authority in key sectors of society has made a huge difference in the weather.

Kopkind and his colleagues seem oblivious to the glaring contradiction in their messages. On the one hand, they boast of the disproportionate influence of the gay community on our culture and our society; on the other, they continue to claim the status of a disadvantaged minority.

This contradiction is reinforced by some of the most recent studies of the gay male population. For instance, last month's unusually thorough survey by the Battelle Research Centers, which attracted so much media attention, showed that homosexual experience is forty times more common among those who hold college degrees than among those who never completed high school, and that exclusive gay orientation is skewed similarly in the direction of the more-educated respondents.

Even more striking are the numbers gathered by Simmons Market Research concerning the 200,000 readers of *The Advocate,* the nation's leading gay magazine. Those readers boast an average annual income of $62,000—nearly twice the national average. They are also more than twice as likely to own a CD player, and twenty times more likely to have vacationed abroad in the last three years.

While gays can certainly be found in every walk of life and in all economic strata, statistics suggest that as a group they occupy a relatively privileged position in society. No one can deny the existence of gay janitors and welfare recipients, but the homosexual population is unquestionably concentrated in the professions, the arts, academia, the media, and other influential elites.

If any strictly enforced quota system were applied to these fields, based upon percentages of sexual orientation in the general population, it would surely hurt—rather than help—the gay community.

In discussing this question with one of my gay colleagues, he freely acknowledged that homosexuals represent a disproportionately prosperous sub-group within the society, and he believes that a process of self-selection helps to explain the situation. According to his reasoning, the more educated, artistic, and sophisticated you happen to be, the less likelihood there is that you will succumb to homophobic attitudes—and therefore you will be more likely to recognize and accept your own gay impulses. This argument, however, would be anathema to most gay activists because it posits an uncomfortable element of volition, of informed choice, when it comes to defining sexual orientation.

However one explains the remarkable achievements of a community that is so relatively small (no matter whose numbers you accept), the prestige and prosperity of so many homosexuals highlights the way that their current push for "equal justice" is fundamentally different from other civil-rights struggles of recent years.

The gay-rights agenda includes no affirmative-action demands because that agenda is not focused on economic opportunity or access to the establishment. It concentrates, rather, on winning acceptance and respect for those who choose to live their lives openly as homosexuals. The most pressing demands involve a change in private attitudes, rather than an increase in practical opportunities.

The fact that the gay-rights movement is fundamentally and profoundly different from previous advocacy campaigns by other embattled minorities doesn't necessarily make its aims invalid. But it does suggest that homosexual activists confuse public discourse and undermine their own credibility when they try to downplay the unique and unprecedented nature of the controversial mass movement they have launched.

TRUE PERVERSION

Stan Leventhal

One of the more perverse aspects of the increasing mainstream media coverage of queer culture and politics is the huge gap between reality and perception. As more independently distributed books and films illuminate all the shadowy realms of life as we know it, the commercial media—and its henchpersons—still attempt to obscure the cold, hard truths. Lies and misinformation not only get a hearing, but become recycled by journalists and broadcasters who are too lazy or ignorant to get the facts.

In the guise of concern and compassion, Michael Medved writes about affirmative action and the gay community, and one can only wonder why this writer is begging an argument. To make a big deal of a nonissue is surely an attention-grabbing device that only a desperate, ill-advised reporter would attempt. But it does nothing to clarify the real problems facing mainstream America; it only adds to its rampant homophobia. It is unfortunate that with all of the accurate information available regarding the queer people of America, most people's ideas and opinions are shaped by media bias. And many believe that what they are being told is the truth, so they are not motivated to look any further, dig any deeper. It is apparent that Medved knows nothing about gay culture or the queer community, nor does he seem to have much awareness of minority cultures in general. For him to lump together all of America's minorities and simplistically ignore the vast differences in their problems and goals calls into question not only his ability, but the ability of the editor and publisher who provide his forum.

The reason why affirmative action is not of concern to gays is because many of us are invisible. Most African-Americans and other people of color do not have that option. Sad that Medved cannot see this distinction, nor the complications which differentiate the needs of lesbians and gay men. Moreover, his claim that there is no need for a gay liberation movement, because some gay people have attained positions of power in certain professions obscures the fact that gays who have made significant contributions in the arts are only a small percentage of the overall gay population and mostly male; that the gays who become prominent politically have only as much clout as the media allows; and that most gay people lead ordinary lives and constantly have problems with their jobs, apartments, and homes, with the general mood of homophobia which permeates all areas of American life. Because Medved can point to a few successful gay people does not mean that we don't have major problems that need to be solved.

I wonder if Medved has ever read anything by Randy Shilts, Lillian Faderman, Sarah Schulman, Harlan Greene, Jewelle Gomez, Martin Duberman, Randall Kenan, Michael Nava or Dorothy Allison. Or whether he's ever talked to any openly gay people. The difference between Medved and a writer with principles is that those who know nothing about nuclear reactors, for example, don't expect to see their opinions on them in print. He, however, has no trouble broadcasting his ignorance; he is obviously unconcerned with just how much damage more media misinformation can engender. If he had any integrity, he would stick to writing about Schwarzenegger and Stallone movies, a job which requires very little in the way of truth or knowledge.

THE EROTIC ELEVEN

Bobby Lilly

I attended the 1993 Las Vegas Consumer Electronic Show (CES) last January with my spouses, Dave and Nina Hartley. As an adult actress, Nina had a full schedule that week; but she volunteered to perform at a benefit to raise money for the adult industry's battle against censorship.

The benefit, a lingerie show, was held for the third year in a row at the Pure Pleasure Video Store. Admission was the purchase of a ten-dollar raffle ticket which could be used for any raffle that evening. Additional tickets could also be purchased. Performers modeled lingerie donated by the store, and there was a special gimmick. Winners claimed their lingerie by peeling it off the star's body with their teeth, hands behind their backs at all times.

On Friday night Nina attended a rehearsal for the Adult Video News Awards (she was presenting), then went straight to the benefit. About 11:30 that night, the phone rang in our room; it was a close friend who had gone to the benefit. The first words out of his mouth were "Bobby, I want you to know everything's okay and Nina's all right." My heart stopped. Suddenly, my imagination raced out of control and images of freak accidents flashed before my eyes. I almost missed his next words: "The show was busted and Nina's been arrested along with everyone else."

Dave immediately headed to the police station. I waited for calls. When Dave finally checked back, I learned that the eleven performers still at the show (several women had already left) had been arrested and charged with open and gross lewdness, conspiracy to commit prostitution, and soliciting prostitution (all misdemeanor charges). The women charged were Nina Hartley, Sharon Mitchell, Patricia Kennedy, Trixi Tyler, Beatrice Valle, Nina Suave, Lacy Rose, Shalene, Danielle Cheeks, Ari, and Naughty Angel.

Bill Margold, head of Fans of X-rated Entertainment (FOXE) and the benefit's promoter, was arrested along with the bookstore owner. Seymour Butts, who had videotaped the show, was also arrested. They were charged with multiple counts of felony pandering and receiving money from a prostitute.

The arrests were made only after at least six police officers sat through four hours of live performances. Apparently, they had nothing better to do! They could have stopped the show at any time. Yet, when Captain Ron Niemann, commander of the vice detail, was asked why his detectives didn't act sooner, he was quoted in the *Las Vegas Review Journal* as saying, "I'm not going to even respond to that. That's stupid. If we had stopped earlier, we wouldn't have gotten all the suspects, would we have?"

Niemann did not explain why, even though fifteen women had performed, only the eleven women present at the end of the evening were ever arrested or charged. Nor did he mention why none of the men from the audience who had gotten onstage with the women had been arrested. To me, that smacks of sexism and gender discrimination. I am outraged that the police targeted such a benefit. Who was being hurt? Where was the harm to society?

I have been asked what *really* happened that night and have to answer truthfully. I don't know. I wasn't there. However, some of the stories I read in the adult press gave the impression that the event was a wild sex orgy where the performers were kept busy servicing the men in the audience one after another throughout the show. True? I strongly doubt it.

Reports I heard said several women got carried away onstage and had essentially "woman handled" a couple of the men from the audience. I was also told that the women had only simulated activity with these men. The only consistent story I got from people who were in the audience is that most of the women appeared to be "playing" with each other. Simulated activity or real—I don't know. Nina herself gave a lecture on how to make love to a woman while two friends demonstrated the techniques she described.

Perhaps some of these women did step beyond the bounds of propriety during their performances, but charges of prostitution were totally inappropriate and nothing more than an attempt to hurt and discredit all of them. The police knew *they were performing at a benefit* and should have known that they had volunteered to appear onstage that evening. The police had no evidence that the women were paid for *anything* they did that night, but justified the wholesale prostitution charges by theorizing that the purchase of raffle tickets at the time of admission was actually payment for sexual favors. They also insinuated to the press that deals were made ahead of time to rig the raffles. A ludicrous idea if I ever heard one. While the fantasy of appearing onstage with an adult video star may be stimulating, the reality of stepping in front of eight hundred men who are watching every move you make is terrifying. I can't imagine anyone paying for that experience. Talk about performance anxiety!

I have become a defense coordinator for the women (they have a different lawyer from the men because of possible conflicts of interest) and have been working closely with their attorney, Dominic Gentile. I started a defense fund called The

Freedom Fund to cover the actresses' legal fees and expenses. I promised Margold and Butts that, if I raised enough money for the women, I would try to help them as well, but said my first priority was the women.

Arraignments were scheduled for early February 1993 but were then postponed. Deputy District Attorney John Lukens, head of the city's sexual assault unit, was assigned to this case after asking specifically for it (something that is normally never done). He decided to drop the original misdemeanor charges against the women and, instead, filed felony charges with the Clark County grand jury under Nevada's ICAN statute, an archaic law which criminalizes all same-sex sexual activity (even in private), and defines such contact as "an infamous crime against nature." It carries a penalty of up to six years in prison.

Obviously, this case has been politicized. Vegas has decided to clean up its "Sin City" image and become more family oriented. And, Vegas politicians were out to make an example of these women to ensure that this would *never* happen again.

Butts, the videographer who taped the show, voluntarily appeared before the grand jury and turned over his tapes of the event. Charges against him were dropped, but on February 26 indictments were handed down against everyone else. The store owner and Margold (who also emceed the show) still face multiple counts of pandering. Ten women were each indicted for two counts of "felony lesbianism" for violating Nevada's ICAN statute and face up to twelve years in jail. One count was for being the active partner and the other for accepting the attentions of her partner. Nina was charged with one count of pandering for "...unlawfully, willfully, knowingly and feloniously... [encouraging two women] to continue to engage in prostitution by soliciting money from male patrons...."

Nina is my "wife." Both on a personal and a political level, I am appalled that she was singled out for pandering when all that she did was give a lecture on how to make love to a woman. I believe that singling her out in this way was done deliberately to attack this high-profile crusader against censorship and discredit her and her cause in the public's eye.

Why did Lukens drop the prostitution charges? If he believed these women were engaged in such activity, why did he drop those charges when charging the women with felony lesbianism? Did he believe he could sway a jury more easily to convict them by inflaming homophobic prejudices? When he dropped the prostitution charges, why did he keep the pandering charges? If there was no prostitution, where was the pandering? Explain his logic...if you can.

Watching this case develop as a member of the immediate family of one of the defendants, I find myself living a nightmare that most people will never know. The stress on all of us is unbelievable. The women know they will have to return to Las Vegas time after time before this case is over. But they don't know when—and that makes it difficult to schedule work. Their lives are no longer their own; they are subject to the whims of the Nevada court system.

Caught up in this witch hunt, all of us feel trapped. To stand there helpless, when the power of the state is poised to attack you or someone you love, affects the very fabric of your daily life. The emotional stress has caused all of us to act in ways that are not normal. Meaningless arguments over trivia break out and it takes a great deal of restraint not to let them escalate. The ongoing stress that we are living with drives ordinary thoughts out of our minds; yet life must go on. Everyone's emotions are stretched to the breaking point. At times I find myself close to tears for no rational reason, or losing concentration at times when I need to be focused. The lawyer has become one of the most important persons in our lives. A call from him can make or break our day. All our plans for the next few months are subject to change—and all our plans are dependent on developments in the case.

Because the police gave the real names and home addresses of these women to the press (not a standard practice), several women have been harassed at home by the media. The women feel personally threatened because their real names and the cities in which they live have been printed in papers across the country, and some of the women have obsessive fans.

Arraignment had been scheduled for March 12. According to Nevada state law, all criminal cases must be assigned randomly to a trial judge. However, when our case was assigned, all four of that day's cases wound up with the same judge, Thomas A. Foley, a middle-aged white, conservative Catholic. The odds against this happening were over 38,000–to–1. Was Foley's assignment just a coincidence or was it politically motivated?

When Dominic Gentile, the women's lawyer, learned of Foley's assignment, he took the issue to the Nevada Supreme Court, and the scheduled arraignment was stayed. Oral arguments on the judge's assignment were heard on June 15. As of early July, the court had not issued a ruling on the matter. The women and their families continue to wait—not knowing when the women will be arraigned or when they will finally have their day in court. The uncertainty of the outcome hangs over all our heads. And, too often, helpless to affect the course of events, we can only wait for an end to the suspense. Legal fees are mounting and could easily reach six figures. Meetings with the attorney, court appearances, as well as benefit appearances (all for free, of course) disrupt our lives, and the women have been hurt financially. Nina, like the others, has had to cancel, reschedule, and pass up work because she has to be available. Some of the women have found that they are just not getting as much work as before, and some have been told that clubs are afraid to hire them because of possible police surveillance.

It hasn't helped that the industry itself has not been wholehearted in its support of this case. Some people in the industry are extremely unhappy with the performers and blame them for what happened. They are afraid that this case undermines the adult industry's attempts to gain respectability. How could the women be so stupid as to get themselves into such a situation? One company head reportedly said in a meeting of producers and directors who were discussing the case that, if it were up to him, these women would never work again in the industry. He is not alone in his sentiments.

Unfortunately, none of the women's critics seems to realize that what the women did onstage that night was no different from what they could have done legally in any adult video. While the women may have violated Las Vegas's rules, what they did was nothing to be ashamed of. I know that some critics were reacting automatically to the smear word "prostitution." Others were just worried about the case's notoriety, afraid that it would focus negative attention on the adult-video industry which was already under assault.

Unfortunately, many of the women do not feel a sense of solidarity with the two men still charged. They feel betrayed, misled, and exploited. These women believe that Margold and the store owner misled them about the safe limits in that venue. (Some of the women believe it was done deliberately; others believe it was just incompetence).

These women routinely perform around the country, and they respect the limits of the venues in which they perform. They depend on the club owner or show producer to let them know what is allowed. Unfortunately, Margold and the store owner told the women they could do whatever they felt comfortable doing. And these women have a wide range of comfort regarding public sexuality. I must note that neither man produces such shows on a regular basis, and Bill told me he didn't realize that he had such a responsibility. He said that he had had no problems in the past with other shows, so he didn't expect the police to give him any trouble this time.

For me that's not good enough. People who take a leadership role in the battle against censorship of sexual expression need to think things through more carefully. Anyone producing a high-profile benefit like this one should have checked carefully and known what the community's limits were from the beginning. Flouting the laws should never happen without a clear, deliberate decision to do so. Everyone had the right to know exactly what they were getting into. Performing at a benefit for freedom of expression does not grant people license to do whatever they want. Strategically, this was not a very intelligent way to fight censorship.

Because of this disaster, the chill of self-censorship has settled over FOXE. Their awards show in February 1994 was extremely tame, with no nudity allowed. Fearing that the show might have been targeted by law enforcement, many performers decided not to appear; or, if they performed, were extremely cautious. Bill says that at his next benefit the audience will get close enough to the stars only to throw marshmallows. Hit a star—win a prize.

Anyone who wants to contribute to the women's defense fund can make checks out to The Freedom Fund and mail them to me at 2550 Shattuck Avenue, #51, Berkeley, CA 94704.

ANNIE SPRINKLE
AN INTERVIEW
David Aaron Clark

Annie Sprinkle (a.k.a. Ellen Steinberg, a.k.a. ANYA) is both a cult figure and a cause célèbre for her nearly twenty-year career producing sexually explicit material. One of the first superstars of the original 70s porn era, Annie is still remembered fondly and worshipped rabidly by raincoat-brigade stalwarts who pine over her departure from commercial smut. She has developed a whole new flock of adherents in her current incarnation as a sex-workshop teacher, erotic photographer, and uninhibited performance artist. She performs such shows as Post-Porn Modernist in America and abroad to critical and audience acclaim, and produces radical sex-education tapes such as *Linda/Les Annie—The First Female-to-Male Transsexual Love Story* and the *Sluts and Goddesses Workshop, or How to Be a Sex Goddess in 101 Easy Steps.* A patron saint to the sexually disenfranchised and rebellious, Annie has overcome censorships large and small for her entire career. Shortly after this interview was completed, she called to say that a local printer had refused to print her stationery, which includes an extremely stylized drawing of a bare-breasted Goddess.

G: What was your first experience with censorship? Does it go back to your commercial porn days?
AS: Oh, yeah. I'm thirty-eight. I made my first porno movie when I was nineteen. I was in prostitution when I was eighteen. So that's twenty years ago. During the first dozen porno movies, I became aware that there were things that you could show and couldn't show, you know.

The funny thing is, standards are changing constantly. In the early days, you couldn't do anal. In the beginning, there was always an incest scene and a rape scene in every feature porno movie. Whereas now, rape and incest aren't allowed, but anal sex is. There was a time when golden-shower scenes were perfectly okay. That was when I made *Deep Inside Annie Sprinkle*, which was the number-two best-selling video of 1982. Then, a few years later, the FBI banned that one because of the golden-shower scene.

There used to be a lot more freedom, in a way. I think that what caused the pressure on porn was when the audience expanded from guys in raincoats, the classic porn fan–type guy. Women were not interested in porn. As women became more interested in porn, the "daddies" of the world decided they had to protect their women, or something. Whereas, as long as they were just into it, it was okay. You could do whatever.

So it seems like there's always this pendulum swinging back and forth: freedom, repression; freedom, repression. Being censored is a way of life, a weekly occurrence. That's why this whole thing happened with the NEA, which came about because I performed *[Post-Porn Modernist]* in a government-funded theater (New York City's The Kitchen). It didn't even faze me because I was so used to this kind of thing happening. In retrospect, I think that I should have sent out a press release or done something. But I was too busy making more controversial work.

G: When you were arrested many years ago over *Lover* and *Hate* magazines, where you published your prostitution diaries, it seems they were really trying to censor what you were saying about sex.
AS: When I was younger, I would go to work, several days a week sometimes in a whorehouse. And every day I was being, in a way, censored. What I was doing was illegal, which was absurd to me and made no sense. It was the most blatant case of women not having control over their own bodies, and of this patriarchal system that puts women down and wants to control them. Anyway, it feels like my censorship started when I got into prostitution.

G: So what do you think censorship comes from? Fear of knowledge?
AS: Yeah, partly. It's a way of controlling people. Also, I think that a lot of people are censors because they don't want to be confronted with their own sexuality. They don't want other people to know any more than they know. There's a lot of jealousy. There are people who are terrified of their own sexuality. And so they don't want to walk down the street and see magazines with tits on them because then they're going to think about tits. Add then they're going to think about sex. They don't want to think, they don't want to be confronted with their own sexuality, so they try to control everyone else's.

G: Do you think that's why there have been attempts at censorship of sexually explicit stuff from both the right and the left?
AS: Actually, I see Women Against Pornography as kind of sex workers themselves. They're as much a part of the porn world as porn itself, because they're always busy with it. Their whole lives are based around porn. So is mine. I don't see that it's that different.

G: I'm sure they have a different opinion on that.
AS: My big goal in life is to have sex with Andrea Dworkin. I think she's really hot, a very passionate woman. I'd love to have sex with her. I have a lot of respect for her.

G: What if she calls you up after she sees this?
AS: Well, I have actually invited her to lunch. She didn't really answer one way or the other. But I mean, the fact is the woman gets things done. She's got a lot of power. She's got a lot of ideas. She's absolutely outrageous, and she's always busy with sex. She's very hung up on, very into, really violent imagery. She's pretty wild. She's out there. I see her as very kinky.

G: How about Jesse Helms?
AS: I'd like to spend a weekend with him, too, having sex and playing.

G: Do you think he's just as obsessed?
AS: He's afraid of his own sexuality. He's definitely sexually repressed. But I don't hate people. I'm a lover, not a fighter. I don't hate Jesse Helms. Actually, I love Jesse Helms. I love Andrea Dworkin. I love people who are passionate and doing interesting things around sex. I see it as quite wonderful. Certainly Jesse Helms has sparked more sexually explicit art than anyone else. So I'm very grateful.

The more we talk about sex, the more we think about it, and the more we explore it in the media, the better. These people really inspire a lot of debate and dialogue, energy and excitement.

G: So you don't feel your own personal expression threatened by them?
AS: I don't allow them to have that much power over me. I think people gave Jesse Helms a lot of power. I like to think positively. To go around and be saying that it's worse than ever before, that our freedoms are more likely to be taken away, you're giving power to that whole thought. I say no, we have more freedom than ever. Things are getting better and better.

Because that's the way I see it and that's my experience with it. That empowers my army, my camp.

G: Well, you mentioned changing standards in the straight-sex industry, that there was stuff that happened all the time in the films that now can't be done without fear of being thrown in jail.
AS: I see it kind of like this dance, a tango. It's like being in any kind of relationship. Also, one of the reasons I say that I love Andrea Dworkin and I love Jesse Helms is because I want to teach people how to accept and love people who are different than themselves. I'm trying to set an example to those people on how it could be.

It's so easy just to say, okay, you're different than me, you have different ideas; but I love you and I accept you just the way you are, and I know you're doing the best you can with where you're from and who your parents were and how you grew up. And hey, I'm doing the best I can, and we're different. But isn't it great that we're different? Because you wouldn't want everyone to be like me. I wouldn't want everyone to be like you. So let's just shake hands on it. Let's have fun. Let's have sex together.

G: Before you became so enlightened, was there ever a particular moment of censorship that really angered you?
AS: Yeah, the one time I was put in jail, which was when I was working on *Love* and *Hate* in Rhode Island. We were publishing the diaries I had written while I was working in the whorehouse. We put in an ad for a typesetter. The typesetter turned out to be an undercover policewoman. Here I had finished this labor of love that wasn't even about making money. I wouldn't have made a penny from it. Publish the true stories of my life, which I saw as very wholesome and pure and loving. And these twenty-five state policemen came in with their guns drawn.

They put me in a jail cell, me and my friends. They confiscated everything from my toothpaste to my Tampax, to every photo of my childhood and all my diaries. To actually have someone come and take away my freedom was an amazing experience and pretty terrifying. It was just very surrealistic and bizarre to think that someone felt that they knew better than I did.

I try to keep a positive outlook on things. My job is to keep challenging silly, outmoded taboos, making more work. I'm really happy there are those people out there fighting censorship, saying "We want more freedom," writing letters to the government. But I'm just not one of the fighters. I'm a lover. I am also not stupid. I know that there's some very real danger. Having had my freedom taken away for forty-eight hours, I know what's possible. But if I thought about it too much, I'd just stay in my house. I wouldn't create anything. I wouldn't be doing this interview. So I can't get too involved in what could happen. Let someone else do that, because I have to make it comfortable and safe for me and to keep making sexually explicit work.

G: As someone who's been in both the porn and the art worlds, and done notable work in each, how do you feel about the complaint sometimes raised that the art world only really gets interested in issues of censorship when it applies directly to them? They're upset when a David Wojnarowicz or a Karen Findley gets censored, but they don't quite feel the same when *Deep Throat* or *Deep Inside Annie Sprinkle* is squelched.

AS: I think it's snobbism. If you're born with more artistic skills than Joe Pornographer, should you have more freedom than someone else? I think it's outrageous. It's like that whole argument that only really fine artists are allowed to paint pictures of nude children. Balthus can paint naked little girls because he's a genius. Why should he be any more privileged to explore his sexual desires and explore the way he sees the world than you or I or Joe Pornographer? I'm for everybody being able to make anything they want.

I'm for everyone being able to give feedback. I know for myself, that's how I learn. If I do a performance, I say, okay, I feel this way, so I'm going to show my cervix. I'm going to get feedback from how people react, and I'll learn and grow from that. I see how people have grown through making their porn.

I think that people should be allowed to make whatever it is they want to make and express whatever it is they want to express. But obviously, whatever you do, you take the consequences. If you're going to put out something totally hating Jewish people or something that exploits children, or something hateful, you're gonna get a lot of shit. There are natural laws of cause and effect.

G: When you moved into the art world, did you experience any of that kind of snobbism?
AS: No, the art world's been very, very supportive and welcoming. In fact, I just got my first grant from Art Matters. It felt like a real initiation. But I'm not in the mainstream art world either. I'm kind of on the fringes—where I like it. I've felt much more appreciated in the art world than I ever did in the porno world.

G: Do you think that commercial porn is still pretty much a patriarchal system?
AS: I think just so much porn is boring and stuck in an old rut. But to me the bottom line is prostitution. It's not even about porn, it's about prostitution. I'm a woman, so I could go out and have sex with twenty guys in a day and no one really cares. If I take a few dollars for it to feed my family, then I get thrown in jail and charged and fined. It's ridiculous.

G: What problems have you run into with your sex-education tapes?
AS: The *Sluts and Goddesses Video Workshop* just got censored going to Canada. We've been selling it mail-order and a woman ordered it. It was stopped at the border. Customs said it was degrading to women, and of course the whole point of this video is to empower women. And upgrade them.

G: Did they say what specifically was degrading about it?
AS: No. But the funny thing is, it's played at the most prestigious, partially government-funded experimental video festival in Canada, the Montreal New Film and Video Festival. It got a very good reception there. It's played in Toronto through their arts organization. So it's played there as art, no problem. Hundreds of people have seen it.

G: Then again we have the double standard there. One of the things in that tape is fisting. That's verboten for straight porn these days. They count the number of fingers that go in, and if it's more than three, there's a legal problem. But you've done it in the context of that tape, and this is the only problem you've had with the Canadian border, right?

Sprinkle: Oh, I do have a little bit of fisting, don't I? I don't know if that's why they did it. Actually, you know, it's funny. Each country is different. In England, a journalist reviewing the video wanted a picture of me ejaculating. I have the vibrator on my clitoris when I'm ejaculating, right? Here you can have a vibrator on a clitoris, but you can't show ejaculation. Over there you can show ejaculation, but not the vibrator. How stupid.

They have the funniest laws and ways of censoring stripping, too. Now of course, in a lot of places you can't be topless, so they put latex on the nipples, so you can see the nipples but they're covered. What kind of fucking immature, imbecilic, stupid thing is that? Some judge says you have to cover your nipples. I can't even begin to comprehend the thinking. I could see it if you have to cover them with a bra and not show your breasts. I mean, that somewhat makes sense. But, you know, to cover the nipples with latex... Plus the latex is making all the dancers have sore, irritated nipples.

G: It's almost like a kinky little game. The judge sits there and says, "Oh, you can show me tits, but I need a little something on them, you know, to make it okay."

AS: Yeah. Dominique, my friend, owns a lap-dancing place and she's having to go to court over that. Well, what about toe sucking? Is that prostitution? Can you take money for toe sucking?

In Canada I danced up there and you could show your tits, but you couldn't then take your panties off at the same time. Or, if you took your panties off, you had to have your breasts covered. So what you do is you take your bra off and you show your breasts, and you put your bra back on and then you take your underwear off....

Come to think of it, my first experience with censorship was when I was eighteen. I had my only straight job—well, it wasn't a straight job. My first little job was selling tickets at a movie theater where *Deep Throat* was playing. I was eighteen years old, and this was when *Deep Throat* just came out. It was huge. Hundreds of students from the university, everyone was coming to see it. It was the first porno movie I ever saw. I was like, wow. I had no idea that people fuck on film. I was totally amazed and impressed. I was so surprised. They busted the film, and I had to go to court as a witness. That's where I met Gerard Damiano, who was the director and maker. I became his mistress and met Linda Lovelace.

G: What's your impression of Linda Lovelace?
AS: Oh, I thought she was a goddess. But I think that she obviously was in a relationship with a guy who was very controlling, in what you would call an abusive relationship. I think she loved sex. If you watch her movies, this woman loved sex. I think she had a lot of fun and a good time. And I think she feels really guilty and bad about things. If you read her book (*Ordeal*), she doesn't really blame the porno industry for anything. She really blames this guy. What's to think? I mean, she changed. I think she loved what she did. And then, all of a sudden, she hated it. And now she likes who she became. I think you can change who you are, what you like. I couldn't do what I did ten years ago and be happy now.

G: Do you look at fucking on film?
AS: I can't even look at a porno movie anymore if it's not safe sex. It makes me throw up. I've lost too many friends. I'm too concerned with the future of sex for future generations. I'm very busy creating sex-positive safe-sex information. I want people to learn how to have incredibly fabulous sex safely. It's too painful to watch an eighteen-year-old girl get fucked in the ass without a condom. Because I know if I was eighteen, I would probably be doing the same things as that girl. But as an adult now, I feel responsibility toward youngsters. You know, when you're eighteen, you think you're invincible. When I was eighteen I didn't care if I got a disease. But now, it's life-threatening, and I've just been through too many long, slow, agonizing deaths. So I just started a group called Pornographers Promoting Safe Sex (PPSS).

G: Do you think it's dangerous to be showing that kind of imagery where you have such unsafe sex?
AS: You're telling the public that, hey, here we are, we're porn stars, we fuck all the time, and we don't care about AIDS, why should you. Whereas, if the porn industry started to use more safe sex it'd be like hey, we're porn stars, we're cool, we love sex, we're into it, you know, and we use safe sex. Why don't you be cool, too? They're in the best position to help stop the spread of AIDS. More than any surgeon general, more than any junior high-school teacher, more than anyone else. When the porn stars start using safe sex, people will start using safe sex, too.

G: But you wouldn't want there to be a law that you could only show safe sex.
AS: Absolutely not. If you want to smoke cigarettes, you should be able to smoke cigarettes. I don't think there should be a law. I think that people should be able to make whatever they want to make. I'm not for any kind of censorship, or laws that control what you can or can't do with your own body. I don't like drug laws either.

G: Have you ever seen anything politically, sexually, whatever, that so offended you that you almost wanted to censor it?
AS: No. Actually I love to be offended, or shocked, or to watch really weird things. Personally I'd never want to stop someone from making whatever it is. I have a real hard time with violence as entertainment. I think it's important that people can make it, but I don't go to see violent movies, or wouldn't want to make any except where violence is shown as the nightmare it really is—not glamorize it.

The Sluts and Goddesses Video Workshop, or How to be a Sex Goddess in 101 Easy Steps, a 52-minute video by Annie Sprinkle and Maria Beatty is available for $45 from Beatty, PO Box 435, Prince Street Station, New York, NY 10012.

THE SHAMEFUL ENFORCEMENT OF VIDEO CHASTITY

Joseph P. Cunningham

As I stood at Showtime Video's checkout counter to rent Clive Barker's *Hellraiser* for about the tenth time, I almost missed the petition. It sat in a clutter of movie ads; but once I saw it, my eye was held. A trail of signatures descended below its strong declarative statement:

> WE BELIEVE that the First Amendment gives us the right to watch what we choose in the privacy of our own home. WE RESENT attempts by public officials and others to limit this freedom and control what adults are allowed to watch.

"What's going on?" I asked, tapping the page. The manager, Marge Reidmann, began to ring up my rental and explained that a few people from some local churches had formed a "decency" group a few years ago and had been pushing their moral weight around ever since. Marge had been dealing with it politely and had regarded it as one of her smaller problems until three little old ladies filed complaints with the Cambridge police after their husbands had rented some adult movies.

"Which movies?" I asked as I signed the petition. They were called *Blonde Heat*, *Naughty Lady*, and *So Many Men, So Little Time*. Pretty typical porno titles, really. I rented one in a pointless gesture of defiance, zipped my coat, told Marge to give 'em hell, and headed out into the Minnesota tundra.

For those of you who have been, you know how exhilarating it feels to be idealistic and pissed. This feeling gets especially dizzying when the ideals, which only moments before were completely dormant, come crashing down on you in a storm of fierce tears. I was southbound, doing about seventy with a porno fantasy and Clive Barker's vision of Hell sitting on the seat next to me, when my feelings blindsided me with the realization of just how much I hated what those bastards were doing.

It's not that I'm in love with porno movies. They are, for the most part, a class of films which are almost *traditionally* trashy, the embodiment of the cheap thrill. Good artwork tends to appeal to your emotions and challenge your intellect. All porn does—in fact, all it is *meant* to do—is make you go all warm and stiff (or warm and damp) under your buttonfly. But, as someone once said, knowledge is the birthright of him who seeks it in a free society. Content isn't the point, and no one was forcing this degenerate brand of bad filmmaking onto the decency bunch. The only time they rented it was so they could fuck with everyone else's ability to rent it.

When the East Central Coalition for Decency (ECCD) first got rolling back in 1987, its members' game plan was to write intimidating letters and distribute a list of all businesses in the county which offered pornographic materials for rent or sale. The blacklist would be distributed by Rev. Paul Lundgren, its leader, at showings of an anti-porn propaganda film by Dr. James Dobson, called *A Winnable War*.

Prior to showing the film, the ECCD would send a polite letter to the owner of each business on the blacklist which informed them of their presence on such a list, and that they should "permanently remove the material [before the Dobson film was shown] so that [their] name and business will not be included in the release." Can you say BLACKMAIL, boys and girls?... I thought you could.

I was surprised to learn that this tactic *alone* had worked on two video stores. The other stores, Cambridge Video and Showtime Video, were run by people who apparently, somewhere down the line, had invested in a pair of balls. They had taken an I-believe-in-freedom-of-speech-and-nobody's-gonna-tell-me-how-to run-my-shop stance. The ECCD declared war.

They chose Cambridge Video first because a small mom-and-pop operation is financially vulnerable. In April 1990, three ECCD supporters, probably feeling like undercover operatives on a mission from God, rented a few XXX movies and promptly filed complaints with police the next day, using a prefabricated form supplied by the Clean Up Project of Minnesota, a religious right-wing group that pumps out a lot of pamphlets and tracts on how to rid your town of filth in ten easy steps.

Complaint filing isn't a big deal unless you've got Gary Lambert for a police chief. Dennis Coleman, the owner of Cambridge Video, was popped with a search warrant in May 1990. This was done quietly, and the local paper never covered it (Lambert, it seems, filled Mr. Coleman in on the wisdom of a shut mouth). This becomes all the more sickening when you realize that the warrant authorized the seizure of records revealing the names of those who had rented X-rated tapes.

One of the things taken in the raid was a movie called *Exposed*. What follows is an excerpt from Chief Lambert's official police report, which describes the content of the videotape:

Scene 33

Cheerleader is in Willies [sic], (coaches) office. She asks him

> if this is how she will really get to be head cheerleader (she is kissing and sucking his penis)?
>
> Willis bends her over a desk/pulls down her panties [and] then sticks his penis into her vagina... She rides his penis.
>
> Scene 34
>
> He now masturbates into her mouth. She sucks on his penis. She then "Deep Throats" him a couple of times. Then he wipes some cum [sic] off of her face with his finger, and places it in her mouth.

Lambert later wrote a letter to Coleman, in which he said, "Please do not make [this film] available to the people of Isanti County.... If you do not immediately pull this film from your store, further action may be taken." And that was the end of adult entertainment at Cambridge Video. Can you say GESTAPO-COP, boys and girls? I thought you could.

I leaped into the fray as this scenario was being replayed at Showtime Video. The search warrant read the same, and Lambert kept true to his Nazi image by seizing the petition. But this time it got him sued. Unlike Coleman, Showtime owner Steve Davis had a bank account big enough to back up his ballsy stance, and he hired the best law firm in the state.

After the local papers ran front-page stories (Davis blew off Lambert's gag rule), Rev. Lundgren published a letter in the *Star* explaining to the public what they were doing and why. A week later, I fired back with my own letter in which I exposed their tactics and went basically ballistic. I even included my phone number so that support could be rallied for the embattled store. While I did have to field a few calls from indignant bluenoses ("But we're trying to *protect* you from this sinful filth!"), the positive response was massive. Over eighty-five people stood up to be counted with Americans Together Against Censorship (ATAC), and my phone rang itself sore for two weeks with calls of support. The wife of a local cop (she withheld her name) even helped out with a suggestion for a new petition.

> We, the undersigned, believe that if the country is going

> to censor citizens' private entertainment, then it should also investigate the private sexual practices of the County Attorney, the Police Chief, and numerous police officers in order to determine if these people might be violating adultery or fornication statutes.

Although we didn't dare use it, we did see to it that the suggestion fell into enemy hands.

That was just a small part of the big noise ATAC made and, while it is difficult to be sure, I feel that the role we played was critical in making censorship in Cambridge a big steamy hit sandwich for the would-be thought police.

Over the next few months, the prosecutor's office stalled, and stalled, and stalled some more until we won, when the obscenity statute was deemed unconstitutionally vague by the Minnesota State Court of Appeals. They were filing on a case in Winona that was almost identical to Davis's.

Last month I paid an unexpected visit to an ECCD prayer meeting. After I shook a few hands and was seated, they prayed for Lambert and other local officials, the video stores owners and their victims and me. There were also prayers for Pat Robertson, James Dobson, Donald Wildmon, Tipper Gore, and Senator Jesse Helms (and *no*, I'm not kidding!).

Then came the great debate, ten versus one. When it became painfully obvious that I wasn't going to convert (I felt like Luke Skywalker resisting Darth Vader's join-me-and-together-we-will-rule-the-universe speech), they gave up and promised to pray for my salvation.

The lesson learned from this entire episode is that censorship doesn't look so savory when it is done in broad daylight and, like all shameful activities, it must be done under the cover of secrecy.

And darkness.

CANDIDA ROYALLE
AN INTERVIEW
Don Vaughan

Actress-cum-producer Candida Royalle may very well be on the forefront of the next great age in adult videos. Her New York-based company, Femme Productions, was one of the first to produce erotica from a truly female perspective, and her target audience—couples—has responded enthusiastically. Over the past eight years, Femme Productions has released seven films, including *Femme, Urban Heat, Christine's Secret, Three Daughters,* and *Rites of Passion*. When the following interview was conducted, Royalle was in postproduction on her eighth movie, *Revelations*, a shot-on-film feature that takes *1984* into the realm of sexual freedom.

Before moving behind the camera, Royalle, forty-two, had a successful career as a featured performer, appearing in such films as *Hot and Saucy Pizza Girls*, *Champagne for Breakfast*, and *Ultra Flesh*.

G: What prompted you to form Femme Productions?
CR: Basically, it came from taking a real hard look at the industry. This really all took place after I had been in the movies. I went into a period of self-exploration and analysis to come to terms with my involvement in the industry and understand why I made the choices I did, being as controversial as it is. What do I think of these movies? Are they bad? Are they exploitive? Do they exploit women? The most important aspect was what I felt about what I had done. In so doing, I came to the conclusion that the concept of adult entertainment is perfectly valid. I think humans have always been curious and interested in looking at one another engaged in sexual activity, but basically [adult films] weren't done with much consciousness or interest in bringing any new information to anyone. They were done for very basic, bottom-line reasons. And that's okay, too, in and of itself, but I thought there was room for exploring the area and its potential in terms of people's relationships and how we relate to one another. I felt they were, indeed, exploitive of women because there was nothing about women's sexuality in them. Women were employed in the making of them, but our sexuality and our fantasies were not addressed one bit.

It got me to thinking, gee...what would it be like to do it from a perspective of more social concern, from a female perspective. So I would say [Femme Productions] came from a few different places. The motivation came from the political challenge, the artistic, and certainly a personal challenge. I was seeing that my name—Candida Royalle—was starting to reemerge with the advent of home video and cable TV, and there was nothing I could do about it. She was going to follow me every place. I also had the desire to use the name myself for something that I could personally benefit from and feel good about. Something I could be proud of. And of course I saw it as a good business venture.

G: How are your films different from traditional adult films? What do you try to add, and what do you try to avoid?
CR: From the beginning, I wanted the focus to be sensuality as opposed to explicit sexuality. Even though these films are explicit, I wanted there to be a lot of attention to sensuality. That builds up to touching, to nuances, to subtlety, to seduction. And I wanted there to be more of a focus on female fantasy and desire, how women like to make love, how they like to be touched. And I wanted there to be a sense of mutuality going on, equal pleasuring, how to really relate to one another in a tender and sexy way. I wanted to see [my films] as a sort of healing between the sexes.

G: Several of your films involve safe sex, specifically the use of condoms. What prompted you to introduce this element, and do you feel it's something your audience can appreciate?
CR: I guess it was after the fourth film, it was on to number five, six, and seven...it was 1986 or 87 and by that time it was blatantly clear there was a real epidemic coming out. I felt, number one: I'm hiring people to engage in sexual activity. The thought of not having them practice safe sex seemed unconscionable. It was like asking them to play Russian roulette for me. In all consciousness, I thought it was too grotesque. If I found out down the line that someone who had once worked for me was now sick, even if I wasn't sure if it was on my set that they contracted it, how could I not wonder and how could I have that on my conscience? So, if they're real-life lovers or they're married, I don't worry about it. But when they're not, I really insist on it. And I've had talent resist.

In addition, I felt that since we are showing people in sexual situations, we have to address the reality. But the way I balance it out is, we don't rub it in people's faces since we're not overly explicit, and we've become even less explicit in our later work—not that I think it's wrong, because I think it's important to show explicit sexuality and genitalia. We're rather phobic about that. I just don't believe in rubbing it in people's faces. And so we can get away with using condoms without people knowing it if it's a fantasy or dream sequence where obviously you're not going to see condoms. But then if it's a situation where...for instance, there's one movie, *Sensual Escape,* where a couple is finally going to make love after they've been dating. It's a real fun piece where you hear all their thoughts and insecurities before they make love. Finally, the man thinks to himself, I feel like a goddamn kid with that condom in my wallet, and he brings it up awkwardly, and you can see that she's actually kind of relieved. Then he makes a little joke about it when he puts it on. Then he says, "I crown you king for a day." Then there's *A Taste of Ambrosia,* which has a scene with a couple who you think pick each other up on the street, but it has a surprise ending. That's the one Veronica Hart did for us. She takes out a black condom and puts it on him and gives him head with the black condom on. It's very sexy. It really shows that the use of a condom can be part of the sexiness. It's a hot scene.

G: I understand your films do not incorporate other aspects such as anal sex. Is that a nod to the AIDS situation as well?
CR: It really is. It's a reaction to a couple of things. That's the one sex act that's so dangerous in terms of spreading AIDS. So what I do instead is shoot a scene to look like it could be anal sex if that's what your fantasy is. I don't have to blatantly show it. And I know I've been successful because someone once said in a review: "She calls herself a feminist but she has anal sex in her movie." And I thought, that's good. That person wanted to see it as anal sex, and that's what they did.

G: Everyone's perspective is different.
CR: Exactly. The other thing is, I remember years ago when I had another mainstream company distribute my stuff, the guy who ran the company said to me: "Oh, Candida, you need more anal sex in your movies." I asked why, and he said, "Because I know who watches these movies. It's husbands who use them to show their wives what they want them to do. Fellatio used to be the thing that wives would never do, so movies were full of fellatio. Now all the wives do fellatio, so they want them to do anal sex." I was horrified at what this guy was saying. He's

telling me to put something in there, not because women want to see it, but because husbands want to get their wives to do it. It was very upsetting to me, and I decided that's not why I'm doing this.

G: How large would you estimate the female audience for adult films is in this country?
CR: I think it's growing. I would say right now it's maybe thirty to forty percent of the market. But we have to respond to it. I think we really need more product to respond to this growth, or we will lose them. But I don't think that's going to happen. I just had lunch with Debbie Sundahl from *On Our Backs*, and we were marveling at how we both feel the women's market and the couples' market is the future. It could be a matter of those few of us doing progressive work getting together hand in hand and creating something strong to answer the market needs more effectively.

G: And you see that as a definite reality in the future?
CR: I really do. I think that women have come out of the closet with their sexuality, and they're going to demand equal time and equal place for their expression. I think Madonna is in that line, and I think that men are going to enjoy this as well. It's going to benefit men so much that there will be a lot of support for it.

G: You've worn a number of hats in this industry, but I'd like to ask you, as a woman, what do you feel turns women off the most when it comes to traditional adult films?
CR: I can't speak for everyone because there are women who like the traditional adult films. I speak a lot from my own personal tastes, from instinct and from what other women say. I think it's really the graphic and ugly depiction... I think it's the ugliness. I don't think women want to see things that are ugly. I think they want to see racy; I think we can get just as raunchy and nasty as any man. But we just don't want ugly. We don't want overlit, gigantic genitalia rubbed in our faces. We don't want big, pimply behinds rubbed in our faces. We don't want lots and lots of

men coming on lots of women's faces. To me, the ugliness of some of this stuff is a reflection of the shame we carry inside of us about sexuality, what our culture has done to us. I think women just want to see it done with a sense of taste and beauty. And again, it's not that we need waves crashing, fade-to-black or romance with roses and sweetness. We can get as down and dirty as anyone. We just want to see it done well.

I remember when I was an actress and I would ask the directors, "Why does it have to look this way, or, why the come-shot scene?" They would always say, "We have to prove it's really happening." And that always sounded like a line of bullshit to me. There are actresses who say they like it, they like the come and this and that, and that's fine. I hate to generalize and say that women have been degraded and used and they are nothing but receptacles because that's sort of the Catharine MacKinnon line. And there are women who like to get down and get into all of that stuff. I just think there's room for more. It's got to move on.

G: Do you feel adult films will ever receive legitimate status? Or do you feel they will always be sort of an underground thing like they are now?
CR: I like to think they will achieve some kind of acceptance and normal status. It's just that it's really going to take an entire change, a shift in our cultural attitudes toward sexuality for that to happen.

G: And you don't foresee that any time in the immediate future?
CR: No. I think they will exist and continue to grow in popularity and legitimacy, but not in any big, tremendous way.

I almost wonder sometimes if there is some unspoken decision to keep sex illicit and that's part of what makes it fun. We've taken sex out of where it just feels good and is a wonderful thing to do and made it into something kind of naughty and bad. And the payoff for that is that's what makes it sexy and fun.

G: I'd like to take a little change in direction here and talk with you about censorship. Let me start by asking you your views on

the growing spate of censorship directed primarily at the adult film industry.
CR: I think there is a lot of fear of sexuality in our culture. I think there's something about keeping sex in a certain place, that sex is acceptable only when shrouded in romance and preferably within the society-condoned relationship of at least monogamy and preferably marriage. I think this is a way to keep things in order, to keep people in their place. Sex without the validation of romance and marriage is really still basically seen as rather illicit in our culture. And open sexual depiction flies right in the face of that. It portrays people openly enjoying sex without anything else attached to it, and in a way that's very anarchistic. I think it could also be seen as very revolutionary, and I think this is considered very threatening to our culture at large. So for that reason it's really seen kind of as an enemy of order.

On the other hand, pornography has always been a favorite, useful tool for politicians. It's a very easy one. It gets people really worked up, and it's a lot easier than discussing things like economic issues, environmental issues—the tougher things. So, in this way I think the censorship movement we're seeing right now is a response to the movement of the fifties and sixties, the open sexuality. I think the conservatives and the religious right are reacting and trying to take back control. And I think the politicians are really jumping on this and using it to boost their personal careers and their campaigns.

G: Has Femme Productions ever been harassed by those looking to censor or ban adult films?
CR: No, thank goodness, we have not been targets at this point.

G: Do you think it's because your films are more couples-oriented and therefore overlooked by the anti-porn factions?
CR: I don't think it's overlooked. I think that what they do is go in stages. They're trying to get the most outrageous and the easiest to prosecute first. And if they succeed, they will just go up the ladder. People like me would be the next target, and then of course anything like *Playboy* and *Penthouse* would be targets, although they have already. And then Hollywood movies and

TV, everything would be cleaned up. But they're starting at the bottom, so to speak. Or the top, however you want to look at it.

I think also Femme Productions doesn't have enough money for them to pay attention to us yet. Have you ever seen the ACLU's report on censorship called *Above the Law?* It details how government prosecutors are operating and who they are intending to go after. These men know they are working above the law, and they basically feel that any sort of nudity and erotic depiction is absolutely objectionable and should be done away with.

What's really telling about all of this, however, is that they are targeting the very big companies, and they are usually walking away with $500,000 to $2 million in damages. That's what they'll sue the company for. With VCA, for example, the owner had to go to prison for a year and pay $2 million. But VCA is still in business. So in a way this is really just extortion, and it's a way for the government to fund its continued attacks on the industry. Since I'm such a tiny company, they can't get any money out of me.

G: So they're just ignoring you?
CR: For the time being. They're probably listening in on us and don't like what I'm saying! (Laughs.)

So how have I responded personally? I've responded to it, number one, with the movie I'm completing now. It's called *Revelations,* and it's about life under the new order. It contrasts the kind of life that could result if people don't wake up with the kind of life that was in terms of sexual expression.

Also, I am responding to it by getting involved with a group called Feminists for Free Expression. We have rounded up a very large number of prominent feminists and written a series of letters to the Senate in protest to the McConnell Bill 1521, and we recently had a very strong letter with all our signatures printed in the *Washington Post* in response to this. We will be continuing as a group to respond to other attempted acts of censorship.

I already discuss these topics in all the interviews I do to try and bring this issue to the forefront because I feel that the majority of the media is not addressing this issue, that they are not reporting it to the people. Not only do I mention it in all the interviews that I can, but I have also helped FFE create a speakers bureau because, in analyzing how the MacKinnons and the Dworkins have gotten such a strong hold, we feel that their technique has been to convince the public and politicians that feminists per se are against sexual depiction and pornography, and are in favor of what can be interpreted as acts of censorship to get women protected. We have got to counter that by showing the public and the politicians that this is not representative of feminist thought. Actually, the majority of feminists are against censorship because we understand that historically it has always hurt women. The best example is a law that was finally passed in Canada that's supposed to protect women. A few months ago, Catharine MacKinnon finally had one of her laws passed. Under it, any materials that were considered objectionable and degrading to women could be taken off the market, banned, censored, sued, prosecuted. And do you know what the very first thing they went after under that law was? They busted a gay and lesbian bookstore because of lesbian-produced erotic depictions. It's really unbelievable. Anyone who really believes these people are out to help women are out of their minds and dreaming.

G: Do you feel the adult film industry has the right to wrap itself in the flag and claim First Amendment protection?
CR: Yeah, I do. It's funny to me, though, because I don't feel there's a political bone in most of these people's bodies (laughs). I think Gloria Leonard is very political, but she's just a small person who is really not reaping much monetary reward from that. But I think that most of those people, while it is their right to do it, it's something they use because it's true. So sure, they have the right. Why not?

G: I'd like to know what your response is to those hard-core feminists who feel all pornography is, by its very nature, anti-woman, and condemn you for participating in the adult film industry.

CR: I think they have a real problem with sexuality in general. I think some of them are very, very frustrated with not having made any progress on certain levels with the women's movement. I think someone like Andrea Dworkin is coming from a place of very deep internal pain from her own experience of abuse. I don't agree, obviously, with what they say. A lot of them will say "Well, just the fact that you're employing women to depict sexual situations is immediately exploitation." Well, then you must think that sex itself is exploitive. I think when you are equally employing a man and a woman to create a sexual situation between two people, there is nothing inherently exploitive about it, unless they really don't want to be there or unless you're forcing one of them to participate in really terrible things. I think [many radical feminists] just can't imagine that a lot of women feel perfectly fine about taking part in these depictions and films, and really some of them even like it. I think this is very, very hard for some people to accept.

G: Why do you feel adult films are still so popular with the general public, despite the actions of those who seek to eliminate them?
CR: I think you just can't kill human spirit, and you can't kill the sexual drive. I think there are a lot of reasons. Our lives are so cluttered with toil and the everyday nonsense of trying to keep our heads above water financially and just get through the day. Then we are encouraged to stay together in long-term monogamous marriages where over time you kind of need a jump start to have good sex every so often. So sometimes it's just one of the only places you can go to for release and to escape the reality of the day-to-day doldrums. You want to have some good sex; you want to stay with your partner. You don't want to stray, so you need a little inspiration. All of these things make a good, sexy movie a very appealing thing once in a while. And people aren't going to give that up. It's reasonable, it's understandable, and in some ways maybe the forbidden quality of it kind of adds to it for people. It's like: This is kind of naughty, but I'm going to go for it. I like doing naughty things.

If it was really something that was so terrible, I think it would go away. But it's not so terrible. It's human nature. We need to have a release on some level. We like to have sex. It's healthy and good for us and we need it in our lives.

G: I'd like to talk with you a little bit about your early career, and I'd like to start by asking you what your feelings are now when you think back on your time in front of the camera. Was it a pleasant experience? Was it educational?
CR: If you worked for decent people, you could feel okay about what you were doing. I can remember working for Dick Aldrich—he always did really funny films. And there was one film, *Hot and Saucy Pizza Girls,* where we had to learn to skateboard. We would ride skateboards to deliver pizzas. And I remember all the girls learning to skateboard in the parking lot of the hotel where we were staying. Laurien Dominique, who has since passed away, was on the film with me, and we had a lot of fun. So there were very nice times.

On the other hand, I would say that the lesser times were when you knew you were working for someone who was just in it for another dollar and didn't have any respect for what he was doing. He would make you feel that way, then. There were also some directors who were not particularly caring or compassionate toward the talent, and I would feel kind of unappreciated and insecure about myself in those situations.

But I really enjoyed the act of filmmaking. There was some glamour to it; it was a creative process. On the other hand, I didn't like how crudely the sex scenes were shot. Some of it was embarrassing to me. I didn't like having lights and cameras shoved up my legs. I didn't understand why it had to be made that way. And I did have ambivalence about what I was doing because of the nature of the way it was done.

G: What projects are you working on now, and what plans do you have to expand and improve your product?
CR: I'm finishing up *Revelations,* which I feel will really turn some heads. It's kind of a *1984*-type story that's about a young married woman who finds a secret cache of erotic materials. It's about how it changes her life and what happens to her as a result. It's really a response to what's going on and a response

to the complacency of the viewers, whom I feel had better wake up and defend their rights to this material, even if they are a little embarrassed about it. I'm looking to grow at this point. I feel very strongly that this is the future. I want to get to be a larger company. I want to bring in other filmmakers to work for me. There are so many gifted filmmakers dying to explore the area of eroticism. They just need an outlet and financing, and I want to provide that. I'd like to become known as a company that provides very good quality, reliable product that respects women and men and is really healing and very positive.

G: What advice would you give someone looking to fight back against censors in their community?
CR: I would suggest that they get on the mailing lists of a couple of different organizations that send out regular mailings about what's going on. For example, the Adult Video Association in California is a good one to support. The address is 270 North Canon Drive, Suite 1370, Beverly Hills, California 90210. Let me also give you the address for my group, Feminists for Free Expression. If anyone would like further information, they can write to us at 2525 Times Square Station, New York, New York 10108. And also, the Media Coalition is really terrific. They send out regular mailings, and they always let people know what's going on. They're at 900 Third Avenue, Suite 1500, New York, NY 10022.

People should also write their senators and representatives and let them know how they feel about these issues. They should try to keep updated on the issues, such as the McConnell Bill 1521, which is so awful, and let their voices be heard. They should try to pick their representatives based on how they vote on these issues. The other thing is, they should understand that there is nothing wrong with what they do, and not feel ashamed to stand up for their interest in good quality sexual materials, and let that be known.

G: How is the Candida Royalle who produced *Three Daughters* different from the Candida Royalle who starred in *Hot and Saucy Pizza Girls*?

CR: She's a woman who has really come into her own. I was a little diamond in the rough back then. It's funny because I always joke now about how the people back then really didn't get the best of me. They should see me now!

I did those in my twenties. I was much more carefree, a touch reckless, a wild, fun-loving young woman. I was just sort of enjoying my twenties and not very serious. I knew when I hit thirty I was getting serious. And I did, indeed, get serious. I got married at twenty-nine, stayed married for about ten years to a very nice man. And I really got my life together. I stopped doing movies shortly afterward because I decided I didn't want to do it anymore. I went into therapy with a wonderful, wonderful woman whom I worked with for many years, and basically pulled my life together. But not because of pornography. My whole life needed work. But I just really pulled myself together and came into my own. I feel I am now a self-assured woman. I appreciate who I am. I have blossomed into someone I can respect, someone that I am comfortable with. I know what I want out of life, and I enjoy life a great deal. I have just as much fun as before, I'm just more serious about my goals. I was a girl then; now I'm a woman.

NUDE, FUCKED, AND FREEZING:

WORKING CONDITIONS OF THE X-RATED ACTOR

Wally Anne Wharton

As a free-lance journalist and showgirl of questionable financial means, I am ever vacillating between studio-sanctified show biz and so-called "pornographic" entertainment. One day I'm selling cereal, and the next day my skimpily clad body. I never linger too long in any one camp; to limit oneself to a single form of exhibitionism would be creative suicide.

What lurks behind mainstream movies and TV? Superstar romance and movie-mogul magic? Try catered meat loaf and trailer life. Between takes actors retreat into their trailers. The bigger the star, the bigger the isolated, brain-deadening trailer.

I haven't seen a trailer once on a sex set. This isn't to say that the end result is better than *Star Wars,* but surely spartan working conditions and the lack of privacy force both cast and crew to kindle a real rapport. Or do they?

Recently I interviewed several horizontal harbingers of heavy breathing on the subject of working conditions in The Underground:

LACY ROSE: I love my work, but sometimes it gets to be a drag if I'm doing a lesbo scene and the other girl's not really into me eating her pussy. I know no matter what I do, I'm turning her off.

NICK EAST: At first I couldn't stand doing anal [sex scenes]. It really grossed me out. I had to shut my eyes and fantasize about something else. Now it's okay. I can get it up for two or three scenes in one day, no problem. That's my job. But I can't come gobs; in fact, I can't even make a woman gag...I like to use a lot of lube. Why not? It makes everything easier. Some actors don't like to use it. It's an ego thing. They're insulted if their partner isn't naturally dripping wet for forty-five minutes.

TIANNA TAYLOR: Once I had to shoot a [video] box cover and it was freezing cold! They sprayed down my red dress with water because the photographer wanted it to cling to my body. Well, it sure did cling; and the cold made my nipples really hard, so the picture turned out great.

BILL MARGOLD: I have the distinction of being the only person ever to stand in for The King, the late great John Holmes. In January of 1977, I was working both as an actor and an agent and I'd hired Holmes for this film *Phantasm Comes Again* in which he's supposed to do two girls in a swimming pool. John calls me from the set, right in the middle of shooting, and says they forgot to heat the pool, so forget it. I rush down to the set; they throw a blond wig on me to try to disguise me as a lifeguard. Then the girls say, "Gee, that first guy was cute, but *this* guy is even cuter!" I get into the pool, the girls go at it, and my body turns completely numb. I get off but don't feel a thing. And my skin turns bright purple. Two weeks later, John actually returned the $250 I'd paid him. That was rare. The King was incredibly cheap.

Aside from occasionally fucking in subzero temperatures, what other health risks must porn performers endure? What about safe sex and the use of condoms? I spoke about this touchy subject with director John D. Player, curator of young talent and creator of the infamous biker-porn series *The Adventures of Dirty Harry.*

JOHN PLAYER: I'm in the business to entertain. My actors have to be willing to take a risk, or they're in the wrong profession. If I go to a circus, I don't want to see the guy on the trapeze tethered to a dozen bungy cords with trampolines and firemen waiting down below and a big balloon tied to his ass. What fun is that?

WW: A balloon tied to his ass might be fun.

PLAYER: You know what I mean. Who wants to see a stuntman doing something that doesn't look dangerous? So if some new actress wants to use rubbers, I say no. Besides, the guy always comes in her face anyway. But if Hypatia Lee wants to use rubbers, she can do what she wants because she's a star and people will still buy her movies. But I *do* make people wear rubbers for anal scenes; getting trich is worse than getting AIDS any day.

I'm about to play a small part in my second John Leslie film, *Anything That Moves.* Get it? I arrive at a run-down Hollywood hip-hop club that looks even more run-down in the harsh daylight. Two hundred feet before the entrance, I'm already tripping over cables. Leslie doesn't shoot on tape, he shoots on film. This makes for a much costlier production and a much longer day for cast and crew.

There's a certain mood on an X-rated set. It's irreverent and high-spirited; it's in-your-ass audacity. It says that the whole world trots off to boring jobs every day while we tape naked women for a living.

I am well-trained talent: First, I check in with the A.D. (assistant director) and production manager. In a Leslie production, even these chores go to adult-entertainment legends like Jamie Gillis and Henri Packard. Gillis growls and smirks characteristically while checking my name off his clipboard. Packard (also co-author of the script) smiles at me myopically and shows me the way to the girls' bathroom which doubles as a dressing room. There is an alcove where the makeup man and hairdresser have set up their hot curlers and paint boxes, but these are only for the principal players—only those who "screw."

Lunch has come and gone, but I notice that a generous table of coffee, snacks and soft drinks remains to placate the extras. So far, conditions seem as adequate as at any "B" movie shoot. However, as I hit the bathroom, I'm met with a glaring reminder that this is a fuck film, not *Masterpiece Theatre.* Scattered all over the floor, on the sink, next to the toilets, is a plethora of Massengill douche paraphernalia and box after box of contraceptive sponges. Evidently the actresses have a safe-sex agenda of their own. Scavenger that I am, I check the expiration date on the Nonoxynol-9 and stuff a couple of unopened sponges into my purse. Hey, you never know.

A strip sequence is filmed, utilizing the many porn-fan extras. These guys may or may not be paid. Some fans will do anything to be near their favorite female performers. Most of them fit the misfit category: wimpy, lonely guys with too much fat and too many problems to handle a real relationship with a woman. I talk to one little guy with a harelip into giving me a picture he's taken of me at the Fans of X-rated Entertainment, or FOXE awards. It's like taking candy from a baby.

Red lights and dry ice simulate a smoke-filled late-night strip joint. A sequined, baby-faced Tracy Winn removes her bra and steps out of her G-string. No music plays as she undulates; that'll be dubbed in later, but her spectators' lust is real.

Originally I was hired for a nonspeaking role, but one of the strippers doesn't show up, so Packard takes a second look at my cleavage and elevates my performing status. I am assigned one unforgettable incomplete sentence: "Kiss, niggers." Before we shoot, I introduce myself to the three other actresses plus Leslie's favorite star, Selena Steele. I remind her that I've met her before on sets and at various awards ceremonies and she warms up a little. Just a little. Selena is a major force in this industry, and she doesn't have to be nice to anyone.

Our scene is full of harsh words, pushing and shoving—even fake blood. After all, watching girls fight is a popular fetish. Leslie blocks our moves and injects us with plenty of energy, but he seems content with mediocre acting abilities. I am "wrapped." Henri Packard beefs up my check for the added contribution. I thank him and leave, eschewing the sex scene. I'm not in the mood to fight the fans for a good view. Plus, shooting a single sex scene to film on 16mm could take several hours.

There's plenty of good, clean sex to see during the F. J. Lincoln production of *Girl Trouble.* This time I'm not acting; I'm merely observing a prominent porn director at work. Taping at Henri Packard's comfortable San Fernando home, I'd feel like I was at a barbecue if it weren't for the huge black cables snaking their way across every inch of the white shag carpet. Lincoln's wife and collaborator, Patti Rhodes, arranges snacks and soft drinks in the kitchen. Actress Heather Hart relaxes in curlers and a bathrobe. Woody Long is joking with the crew. Ebony beauty Dominique Simone plays up her huge green eyes and long light-brown hair that must have washing instructions sewn in the back.

Superstud Marc Wallice collects his gear into a duffel bag and prepares to leave. I make a mad dash to catch him. Wallice is so good-looking that he's an irritant to many male viewers who write in to video magazines to ball-bash him. Any guy that brings out the cattiness in men must be worth meeting. Marc looks and talks like he's never had a rough day in his life, and I mean this in a positive way. I ask for his number and *get it.* What a coup!

Five actresses in various stages of undress and high heels rehearse their orgy, known in the porn world as a "daisy chain." For the next half hour, Lincoln hones his vision of sexual perfection. He's not averse to shooting again and again if he feels that the sequence can be improved upon. As a director, John

Leslie sometimes gets a little irritated at the crew if things don't go his way. Lincoln has the patience of Job.

Finally the girls suck, lick, and plunder each others' bodies with dildos to Lincoln's specifications.

"OOOhhhh, yeah, fuck me baby, heahhhh!!" shouts one tanned, climactic blonde.

"And...cut," says Fred. "Great. Okay, girls, take a break while we set up the next shot."

The girls rush by, flushed and giggly.

"Boy, was that wonderful!" says Lincoln, all smiles as he takes a long sip of water and tosses his wild gray mane. "The blonde was fuckin' her, and then she got off, and then the other girl came. Whoa, that was hot!" Can't he tell they were totally faking it? I hesitate to burst his misconstrued male bubble and instead nod in complete agreement. Spineless, that's what I am.

I return to the set later that evening. Patti Rhodes treats me and a few other industry spectators to a flute of iced champagne. Now this is *my* kind of movie shoot! Scott Mallory, my editor from *Hustler Erotic Video Guide*, is gearing up for his classic portrayal of a male chauvinist pig. He glances at a bare-bones script in between trading one-liners with Fred, Patti, and myself.

Soon Fred and Mal O'Ree are upstairs with the two leading ladies, one of whom is shooting for the very first time. I watch downstairs on the monitor to avoid the unbearably hot lights. The two actresses avenge Mal O'Ree's character's sexist ways by tying him up with their lingerie and making love right in front of him. Mal O'Ree squirms, and the gals rub their sticky bodies up against his helplessly hard cock. That'll teach him who's boss. Why doesn't the women's movement try this one? The neophyte shoves her pink panties in Mal O'Ree's mouth like a gag. Later I find out it was ad-libbed.

It's nearly midnight. Everyone's exhausted and Packard's (now-ex) wife is ragging on everyone to get the hell out of her house. Lincoln remains undaunted, slowly, carefully getting the footage he needs. Finally he presents his two "eating ladies" with huge bouquets of roses and poses for press pictures with a naked girl perched on each of his thighs, holding flowers, beauty-pageant style.

I'm doing a video called *Hung in the Balance*. Gay porn at its finest. As the only woman in an all-male extravaganza, I feel like Carol Channing.

The Trousdale locale is a sprawling late-sixties ranch style with a terrific view of Benedict Canyon. It belongs to an older gay couple—two old queens who made good.

I'm the first to arrive.

"They're going to be a little late," says one of the owners. "They're changing locations." He shows me to a small back bedroom with a spotlessly clean bathroom attached.

I change into my favorite outfit first, in hope that the director will say, "That's fine." I suppose if I didn't bring anything else they'd have to go with my only costume but I like to give the director a choice. Directors love choices. Besides, it makes me look cooperative and it gives me a chance to show off my wardrobe.

An hour later, the crew piles in. Director Hector (not his real name), a sensitive-looking Latino, begins setting the table and speaking in hushed tones to the cameraman. Chicken arrives that we can't eat because it's prop food.

I play Katherine, former wife of could-pass-for-straight Chad who is now living with the overtly gay Tad. Chad invites me for dinner, and I wreak havoc between the two lovers by being bitchy, glib, and still hot for my ex-husband. An X-rated gay *Falcon Crest*.

I emerge from the back bedroom and show Hector my outfit, a low-cut fuchsia spaghetti-strap from Trashy Lingerie. Hector's face clouds while the other actors applaud.

"I figured this is a skin flick, so I'd show some skin," I remark weakly.

"Oh, yes, honey, show it to us!" someone shouts.

"It's wrong for the scene," says Hector. "Let's see what else you've got. And take off some of that eye makeup."

We finally settle on a purple knit suit. Good thing I brought that turtleneck dickey so I can cover up my offensive mammary glands.

I sit down at the table, suddenly very aware of my sex. I decide not to butt into the conversation. The boys are chatting like magpies. Perhaps the only true benefit of being an L.A. actor is hanging out with other actors and talking about how fucked up being an actor is. Prettyboy Chad is living in Malibu with the producer who has a rep for befriending young gay actors. Hmm...

There is a script, but Hector tells me I won't need one. He either feeds us lines or we ad-lib. The actors are amazingly proficient, more so than in straight X productions. Tad has great comic timing and facial expressions. Hector stops us often, very concerned with character motivation and subtext. I feel like an actress again. However, I can tell that leading man Chad is feeling pressured and a little unrehearsed.

"I'm sorry," he says to me. "Can we start again? I keep forgetting your character's name."

"M-my name is Katherine," I warble in my best Parkinsonian Hepburn. "How could you-oo forge-et?"

That breaks the ice. We whale on the scene and have a little time left over to nibble the cold chicken.

I forget my Reeboks and go back the next afternoon to retrieve them. All the guys are literally prancing around in their B.V.D.s. They have just finished a sex scene.

"Oh, Wall!"

"Hi, Wally."

"Hi, guys! I'm just here to get my shoes."

"Listen, Wally," says Hector, squiring me into the conversation pit. "I think you're really good. I have to do a scene for my directing class at UCLA. Would you be in it for me?"

"Sure," I reply, momentarily flattered into forgetting all the hours of unpaid, inconvenient rehearsal ahead.

"Good!" Hector is clearly relieved. We set up a schedule for the following week. Suddenly he looks nervous again. "But please don't tell anyone in the class we did this movie together. I don't want anyone to know I direct porn."

Some malcontents like Hector desperately want to move on to a more legitimate cinematic medium. Others, like Fred Lincoln and John Leslie, wear their scarlet X proudly. To adult-entertainment performers, the drawbacks of a limited budget are secondary to the thrill of having sex on film. Movies, television, straight porn, gay porn: it's all one big show-business carnival. I admire all who participate in any capacity. Those who say, "Watch me sing! Watch me dance! Watch me do a double penetration!" are a rare breed. Maybe not so rare in Hollywood.

SEX, SMEARS, AND FEMINISTS

Bobby Lilly

Andrea Dworkin, Catharine MacKinnon, and I all call ourselves feminists. Dworkin and MacKinnon have been major influences in the development of an "anti-porn" ideology within the feminist movement over the past fifteen years or so; I have long opposed their stand on this issue.

I had hoped that feminism would allow us to examine those aspects of culture that touched on sexuality, structure of the family, and related areas, with clearer eyes and that we would be able to transform our culture into one where sexuality was a positive force in most lives and where monogamy and heterosexuality were not the only acceptable choices. I needed a feminism that would allow for the free exploration of sexuality and alternative life-styles and would support those of us who were explorers in areas that were outside the cultural norm. I needed a nonjudgmental feminism where it would be safe to talk about my life. Unfortunately, in the early 1970s, heterosexuality was viewed with scorn by many lesbian feminists who proclaimed, "Feminism is the theory and lesbianism the practice." Heterosexual women were treated with scorn or pity, and our ideas discounted. In order to remain a part of the feminist community that was being created at that time, many women became lesbians as a conscious political act. In 1972 I had formed a committed partnership with the man I still live with today. I saw myself as a sexual radical living an alternative life-style. Because I refused to deny my sexual need for men in my life, I was forced to remain an outsider to that part of the women's liberation movement. Unless I was willing to sacrifice my sexuality on the altar of political correctness, my voice could not be heard in those circles.

Efforts to fight sexual violence became an important element of feminist activism, and feminists targeted rape, harassment, battery, and incest during this period. There was an explosion of sexual imagery in the culture during the 1970s, and many feminists were outraged at the association of sexuality and violence, whether in pornography or the mainstream media. Unfortunately, these concerns became telescoped into a preoccupation with pornography. Anti-porn feminists began to push the idea that "pornography is the theory, rape is the practice." Andrea Dworkin wrote: "All over this country a new campaign of terrorism and vilification is being waged against us. Fascist propaganda celebrating sexual violence against women is sweeping this land.... Pornography is the propaganda of sexual terrorism."

When feminists like myself tried to defend sexual imagery, we found that anti-porn feminists had redefined the very terms of the debate. Pornography, instead of simply meaning writing and other forms of expression designed and likely to produce sexual arousal, became "the graphic sexually explicit subordination of women, whether in pictures or in words." In her book *Feminism Unmodified*, MacKinnon included this definition of pornography which had originally been authored by Dworkin.

There was a perfunctory attempt to carve out a niche for erotica—sexual imagery which was *not* violent or degrading to women; but, for MacKinnon and Dworkin, commercial sexual images always seemed to fall under their definition of pornography as "inherently degrading" since commercial porn came from a male perspective and was designed for the consumption of men. In their eyes, even *Playboy* was a threat to all women.

In the early 1980s, Dworkin and MacKinnon drafted a model obscenity statute which defined pornography as a violation of women's civil rights. It would have allowed women who claimed to be harmed by pornography to sue the publisher or filmmaker for damages, in spite of the fact that no credible research has ever established a link between sexual imagery and violence. They formed an alliance with right-wing religious fundamentalists to get their ordinance passed first in Minneapolis, where it was immediately vetoed by the mayor, then in Indianapolis. There it was challenged in the courts and voided by the Seventh Circuit Court which ruled it unconstitutional.

Anti-porn feminists didn't care that their allies were both homophobic and anti-sexual and opposed the ERA, reproductive rights, and the women's movement itself. Many feminists, including myself, opposed this ordinance, because we feared its sweeping definition of pornography would silence us, and we knew that it would be used to squelch our expression easily (and perhaps more readily) than anyone else's speech.

On February 24, 1986, the Supreme Court upheld the ruling of the Seventh Circuit Court overturning this ordinance, so the anti-porn forces turned their focus to the right-wing Meese Commission on Pornography as their next-best hope to silence sexually explicit media. Ten anti-porn feminists, including Andrea Dworkin, testified before this committee, and the final report used feminist rhetoric to justify its censorial recommendations.

In July of 1986, partially in response to the Meese Commission, a group of activists from within the sex-positive community of San Francisco founded San Franciscans Against Censorship Together. I was elected to its first steering committee and have been a part of its leadership ever since. Over the years we have grown, and today I am chairperson of a statewide organization now known as Californians Against Censorship Together (CAL-ACT). With CAL-ACT, we have been able to impact the battle against censorship at both the state and national levels during the past six years.

Just as in every other part of this culture, the influence of women has grown in the adult video industry over the past few years and women have begun to produce their own visions of sexuality. Candida Royalle, Annie Sprinkle, Veronica Vera, Gloria Leonard, Brandy Alexandre, Britt Morgan, Sharon Kane, Nina Hartley, Sharon Mitchell, Debbie Sundahl and Ona Zee are only some of the women who have produced and directed adult videos in the last few years. Several women have their own production and distribution companies. Femme Productions, Candida Royalle's company, is known internationally. Within the lesbian community, there are now a number of publications that speak to lesbian sexuality, as well as several video companies owned and operated by lesbians.

Does that please either MacKinnon or Dworkin? Of course not. They continue to try to eliminate all sexual expression from this culture. They even want to protect women when women don't want protection. According to the Video Software Dealers Association, over half of all adult videos are rented by women.

This past year, the Canadian Supreme Court agreed with MacKinnon and changed the definition of obscenity in Canada to one based on "harm" to women. The very first seizure of material under this new definition was the lesbian sex magazine *Bad Attitude* which was taken from Glad Day, a lesbian and gay bookstore in Toronto.

In Massachusetts, the state legislature has been considering MacKinnon/Dworkinite legislation to "protect" the civil rights of women and children.

In the U.S. Senate, S.1521 (The Pornography Victims Compensation Act) sponsored by conservatives and supported by anti-porn feminists as well as the religious right, was passed by the Senate Judiciary Committee. It died in 1992 because of pressure from First Amendment activists and feminists, including FACT; California State, New York State, and Vermont State National Organization for Women (NOW); and a new group called Feminists for Free Expression (FFE). These feminists' efforts kept this legislation from being sent to the floor of the Senate. They couldn't stomach the idea that this bill would allow rapists and batterers to evade responsibility for their actions by claiming that "Porn made me do it," perhaps even allowing them to use it as a legal defense.

MacKinnon calls women who oppose her "house niggers who sided with the masters." During the debate over S.1521 she and Dworkin refused to appear on TV shows with feminists who opposed their position, effectively silencing the voices of their feminist opponents by allowing no debate on the issue to take place.

These two have always claimed they are not censors, that they are concerned only with protecting women from the "harm" of pornography. However, a recent incident in Ann Arbor, Michigan, exposes the hypocrisy of such a position. MacKinnon, a law professor at the University of Michigan, had obtained funding for a new law journal titled *Michigan Journal of Gender and Law,* as well as a symposium titled *Prostitution: From Academia to Activism.*

Andrea Dworkin, John Stoltenberg (a New York writer), and Evelina Giobbe (director of WHISPER, an anti-prostitution group from St. Paul, Minnesota) were among the invited speakers. Despite the fact that the symposia were held at a major public university, all the invited speakers believed, as did MacKinnon and Dworkin, that prostitution should be eliminated from society because it degrades women, incites sexual violence, and violates women's civil rights. According to an article in *The New York Times,* one of the student organizers said, "We had a problem as soon as we invited speakers, because some of the key anti-prostitution people accepted on the condition that they wouldn't speak if there were people from the other side there. We agonized about it because we felt we were being manipulated, but we went ahead anyway."

In order to offset the one-sided perspective of these symposia, student organizers of this three-day event invited Michigan artist Carol Jacobsen to curate an exhibit titled *Porn Imagery: Picturing Prostitutes.* According to one of them, "Part of the reason we wanted Carol Jacobsen's exhibit so much was to show the other side, without confrontation." The exhibit contained the works of seven artists. The artists were Paula Allen, Veronica Vera (former adult actress and prostitute), Carol Leigh (a.k.a. Scarlot Harlot), Susanna Aiken, Carlos Aparicio, and Randy Barbados, as well as Jacobsen herself. Jacobsen has been an outspoken critic of MacKinnon's anti-pornography views and supports abolishing laws criminalizing prostitution.

Part of the exhibit had been on display for a week and, when the conference began, Jacobsen installed a two-hour videotape featuring five works, including Veronica Vera's *Portrait of a Sexual Evolutionary,* which included footage from sex films, photos from magazines, and a brief clip of her testifying against an anti-pornography measure before the U.S. Senate, as well as Carol Leigh's video, *End Poverty, Not Prostitution.*

The next morning the videotape was removed by a group of law students from the journal staff, who said they were acting in response to complaints by two of the speakers, Stoltenberg and Giobbe. According to one of the students, "We really didn't think of it as a censorship issue but as a safety issue, because two of our speakers said that, based on their experience at other events, the tape would be a threat to their safety.... It wasn't our place to assess that threat. It was our position to trust our speakers. Seven of us from the journal made the decision to remove the tape, and I regret that it made people unhappy. I don't regret the decision."

When Jacobsen discovered the tape missing, she assumed that it had been stolen and installed a second copy. When she found out what had happened, she discussed the issue with the student organizers. "I told them they couldn't just pick out selected artwork and remove it from the exhibit, but they didn't seem to get it....They said it wasn't censorship; they were just trying to protect people from getting their feelings upset. I said if they wished to censor any part they would have to censor the whole thing. They came back and said, 'Take it down.' And that's what happened."

MacKinnon, stressing that she was not involved in the decision to pull the video, said that she supported the students' action. "It is one thing to talk about trafficking women, and it is another thing to traffic women," she said. "There is nothing in the First Amendment to require that this school, or students in it, be forced to traffic women. If these materials are pornography—and I haven't seen them so I can't say—it is not a question of their offensiveness, but of safety and equality for women. Showing pornography sets women up for harassment and rape."

Less than a month later, at a regular meeting of the California State NOW Board (of which I am a member), anti-porn activists attempted to change the board's position opposing S.1521, the "Pornography Victims' Compensation Act." Among the materials they handed out was a partial copy of an article in *Spectator Magazine*, a Bay Area adult publication. I had written about a 1990 "Take Back the Night" March in San Francisco. My picture was displayed prominently, but the text of the article was blurred and illegible, except where I had used the term the "Dworkinite deformation of feminism." I had written that I was using this term to describe the sex-negative position of feminists led by Dworkin. 'Sex-negative' was heavily underlined by these women. I was referred to as a "reporter" for the *Spectator* (which I am not) during the presentation of their position while they held up my article which was titled "Sex-Positive Feminists Take Back the Night."

Several times they emphasized that women opposing the bill were doing it only out of economic self-interest, each time glaring balefully in my direction.

Later they passed out photocopies of bondage images and cheap paperback books with titles that implied violence and incest. Scrawled in red over these images were the words "sex-positive feminism" over and over again.

The board was not swayed by their theatrics. I have always been open about who I am, so no one on the board was shocked at the thought of my writing appearing in an adult publication or that I might have connections to the world of "porn."

I ask you: Which side of this feminist debate is really trying to smear and silence which side?

THE MASTUR RACE:
AN INTERVIEW WITH DIAN HANSON
Mark Kramer

Pornographer Dian Hanson's adventures in the skin trade span the almost two decades that have elapsed between the age of porno chic and today's devitalized era of sexually transmitted death. As editrix of such popular newsstand magazines as the mammocentric *Juggs* and *Bust Out, Leg Show* and—until recently—*Big Butt,* Hanson is widely regarded as the doyenne of anatomically specific smut. In a field where anonymity is generally prized by purveyors and consumers alike, the buxom, Brunhildesque, fortysomething Hanson has generated a widespread cult following through an intimate—albeit epistolary—dialogue with her readership. Dian Hanson's mailbag is an embarrassment of raunchy riches that totals thousands of reader-written letters each year, and it has afforded her an almost preternatural insight into the obsessions that send raving the race of men. In this exclusive *Gauntlet* interview, Hanson discourses on sex, sin, and the culture of masturbation.

G: How did you make the transition from respiratory therapist to pornographer?
DH: Well, I always liked pornography. I was interested in pornography from the first time I saw it, which was down in the furnace room where my father kept his stash. My brother and I used to sneak down there and look at it. We'd find it wherever it was hidden. I was always curious to see whatever it was I wasn't supposed to see. But I was also extremely curious about the human body. And about animal sex. I lived out in the country. Animal sex was very exciting. I knew something very powerful was going on there. Here was your own pet dog, who was very predictable and normal, and then sex would enter in, and he'd become this other creature: he'd be slobbering and barking and acting very strange. It became evident to me that sex could completely transport a being into another world. And that could not escape a child's attention. When I was seventeen or so, I saw my first really hard-core pornography, and it just absolutely riveted my attention. I couldn't believe it. It was really exciting to me, and I just wanted more. I wanted to buy my own pornography. And when I turned eighteen, and then could legally buy pornography in Seattle, which is where I grew up, I took the birthday money which my mother sent me (I was an emancipated child living in another state from my parents) I went right down to the "adult" bookstore and bought hard-core pornography.

G: What was the first porn mag you bought?
DH: It wasn't a magazine. It was the illustrated *President's Report on Obscenity and Pornography* from Greenleaf Classics, which was just a ploy to show everything we're not allowed to talk about: bondage, SM, gay sex, straight sex, everything. I loved it. So I always sexualized everything. I was a respiratory therapist, but I was always the one who was getting in trouble for thinking

about sex, talking about sex, contriving to peek under the sheets to look at the patients naked, noticing if a patient got an erection, and always wanting to talk about it. So I always had a reputation for being sexually obsessed. And when somebody I knew got the opportunity in 1976 to start a sex magazine, which was *Puritan,* I was eager to hop aboard and work in pornography.

G: *Puritan* seemed notable for its attempt to balance "name" writers with quality art direction....
DH: There was an interview with Norman Mailer. To their credit, they decided to do just hard-core, and were so pretentious about it that they were able to get these name writers. The late Marco Vassi was one of our staff members. It was really started with the kind of misguided notion—this was in 1976—that things were getting more and more open. This was the year of the greatest openness on the national newsstands. Magazines like *Cheri,* which came out the same year, were actually showing finger insertions. They were showing women pissing. They were showing things that you never see anymore. And the people who started *Puritan,* who were watching this progression, thought that the next thing was going to be open hard-core on the newsstand, and they were going to be the first to do that. And of course, as we know, that never happened. It's gone steadily back the other way—which most people aren't aware of, because pornography as a social evil is such a beloved subject to American politicians who want us to think that pornography is getting ever more explicit and violent and vicious. Whereas the truth is that ever since 1976 the censors have drawn the noose tighter and tighter around our necks until we can hardly put anything in sex magazines. We can't even use the word "rape," let alone show imagery of it. We can't acknowledge that people have sexual urges under the age of eighteen—not even in letters written by readers. Details such as being aroused by a teacher in the sixth grade—that just doesn't happen in the world of American pornography, because, Lord knows, if we write about something like that somebody might think that a sixth-grade boy gets aroused by his teacher and then...who knows what the boy

might do? There's that fabled connection between normal sexual urges and violence. I don't know where that came from. But that's another one of the myths that's propagated in our country. It puts politicians in office and keeps them there.

G: Child pornography seems to have taken on a mythical, folkloric dimension, along with vanishing hitchhikers and mice in Coke bottles. But there's actually very little reality behind the hysteria. Isn't it true that the only child pornography being produced in America today comes from the federal postal authorities?
DH: By the postal authorities and by European countries. It's produced in Amsterdam, although it's just become officially illegal there. And it is produced in Scandinavian countries—very, very small quantities of it. People will say, "You pornographers don't want to admit that child pornography is being created." But let's look at it cost effectively: besides the fact that most pornographers are as morally repelled by the exploitation of children as any other Americans, how many people do you know who are turned on by prepubescent children? There aren't very many. It's not like this is the common thing, that everyone in the United States is saying, "We're turned on by prepubescent children, but we'll take women with huge breasts since we can't get children." It's a very small group of people who are interested in this material. Meanwhile, the penalties for producing this material are immense, while the amount of money to be made by producing and selling it is infinitesimal. It's tiny. So it's not cost effective for any pornographer—for anyone who wants to make money from pornography—to produce child pornography. It just doesn't make sense. And so it's not done. If people thought about it logically, this would occur to them. But nobody does because you can't say the words "child pornography" without everybody screaming hysterically and rushing around hitting you.

So it never gets discussed, and they don't want it discussed, because, once again, we need an enemy. We don't have communists anymore, so now we have these enemies within: child pornography and drug abuse.

G: What is the psychographic profile of the average American masturbator?

DH: Virtually every American man is a masturbator. Ninety-eight percent of American men masturbate throughout life, from puberty or pre-puberty to the grave. But if you're talking about a person who masturbates in preference to interpersonal sex—certainly a lot of my readers fall into this category. I encourage my readers to write to me about their masturbation practices and to be open about their masturbation practices and to feel more at ease and less ashamed about being masturbators. I find they often come from very rigid, often religious households. They're taught at an early age that all sex is sin. And masturbation is much safer. They often grow up with parents who do not give an inspiring example of married life. Their parents fight a lot. Maybe the father's a drunk. Maybe their mother's overbearing. Maybe they're beaten. They don't want to grow up and repeat what their parents have. They look at that relationship, and marriage and family life don't look very appealing to them. They'd rather not get that close to a woman. It's frightening to get that close to a woman because then they might repeat what their parents had. And, anyway, they're looking at the average American once again—and most of us grow up in dysfunctional families. But I think those are a couple of elements: somebody who learns at an early age that sex is "bad," and marriage and family life are frightening.

G: So...do you feel that society benefits from the abundance of masturbatory opportunities available today?

DH: Pornography and the proliferation of pornography is a sign of our becoming more civilized. People today have the leisure time to explore and enjoy their sexuality. Most men biologically have a higher sex drive than most women. Being visually oriented, they're more easily aroused, but also more easily satisfied. Men satisfying their greater desires through masturbation, providing themselves the variety they crave through pornographic fantasy, is far more civilized than coercing or cajoling uninterested women.

G: When one invokes the category of "Women in Pornography," the names that come up are Dian Hanson, Candida Royalle, and Annie Sprinkle. And on the male side, there's Al Goldstein. It seems as if there's no one, other than the usual suspects, willing to speak on behalf of—or identify with—pornography anymore....

DH: This has to do with the absolute national shame about sex. How come we don't have an institute of sexuality? How come there is nowhere in the United States an institution whose sole concern is American sexuality?

G: The Kinsey Institute...?

DH: The Kinsey Institute is a gathering of objects. They take your diaries, they take your dildos, they take your pictures—you can get a tax write-off if you send them that stuff. I know people who do it every year. Photographers who send them all their outtakes, and they get a write-off for giving to the Kinsey Institute. It's just a museum. But they're not dealing with people's problems. If a person, a young man, say, finds himself compelled to dress up in his mother's clothes and put a noose around his neck—and we know that this isn't an uncommon thing—where does he go for help?

G: Oprah?

DH: There should be an 800-number! It should be up in the subway! "Are you worried about your sexual urges? Call this number." And you'd have real people who understand this stuff talk to the person and help him. Or they can write to me—describe it in detail. And send photographs. (Laughter.)

PORNOGRAPHY'S VICTIMS

Phyllis Schlafly

It's a funny thing, when the subject of pornography comes up. It generally seems to be discussed within the framework of two competing rights: the right of the seller and the right of the buyer. That's like discussing drunk driving only in terms of the right of the tavern to sell alcohol and the right of the drinker to buy it.

Unfortunately, there is a third party to the equation: the victim. Just as the rights of victims of drunk drivers need to be considered, so also we must consider pornography's victims. Identification of this third party was one of the major achievements of the Attorney General's Commission on Pornography. Its 3,000 pages of hearings in 1985–86 for the first time gave pornography's victims the opportunity to present their side of the story.

The complete hearings were not published, so few people ever heard what the victims had to say. The 2,000-page Report of the Commission included a few excerpts, but that thirty-five dollar book was not carried by bookstores, is not widely available, and is too formidable for many to tackle. Anyone who takes the time to read the 3,000 pages of hearings will acquire a view of pornography quite different from that circulated by the American Civil Liberties Union, People for the American Way, and other advocates of the right to sell and buy porn.

The eyewitness testimonies of those who spoke at the commission hearings prove that pornography is an addictive and corrosive element in our society today. Those who are raped, tortured, and killed by pornography's users are only a small percentage of pornography's victims.

It is self-evident that the victims of hard drugs are not limited to those who kill and are killed under the influence. Illegal drugs also destroy the lives, health, and relationships of all who use them. Likewise with pornography. The firsthand testimonies of the witnesses show how pornography starts with playful experimentation, then becomes addictive, then changes men's attitudes toward women and sex, and finally destroys their personal and sexual relationships.

With some men, their addiction leads them from the risqué to the perverted and bizarre. With some men, their addiction leads them into physical abuse of their wives and other women, and into seduction and sexual abuse of children.

With most of pornography's addicts, however, probably the biggest effect is their change of attitudes toward women. Until the 1986 Commission on Pornography, that harm was unseen because the wives were silent, too embarrassed to go public, too hurt to share their grief.

The hard-core and violent porn convinces violence-prone men that violence is part of the normal male-female sexual relations, that women desire and enjoy rape, and that rape is only the exuberance of an oversexed man. The soft-core erotica convinces nonviolent men that women (and often children, too) are inanimate toys for men to play with and use for their own satisfaction. That's the way women's bodies are presented in the "men's entertainment" magazines.

Through the vivid color pictures of television, video, and slick magazines, pornography teaches the falsehood that women enjoy being sexually used; despite the obvious pain and degradation, there is always that smile on their faces. Logic and reason cannot erase those pictures in the man's consciousness. The pornography addict loses all personal relationship with his sex partner. The porn pictures have convinced his subconscious that the woman probably enjoys whatever he does, and in any event he doesn't have to be concerned about her response because she's just an object.

The law of obscenity tries to distinguish between hard-core and soft-core pornography, and many people try to distinguish between violent pornography and erotica. But to the wife-victim of the porn addict, that's a distinction without a difference. Witness after witness told how this change in men's attitudes took place primarily as a result of the magazines easily available at local newsstands and convenience stores, now massively reinforced by television, porn channels on cable, and videos for rent. The $8 billion pornography industry is now so pervasive that men no longer have to go across town to adult bookstores or movie houses to feed their addiction.

All Americans enjoy a freedom-of-speech right to express racist attitudes, but they are clearly socially unacceptable today. The time has come to recognize that pornography, even when it's not legally prosecutable, is socially UNacceptable because it victimizes women and children.

Here are a few of the testimonies of the victims who gave their firsthand stories at the 1986 hearings of the Attorney General's Commission on Pornography.

Sharon met her husband at college where she received her B.S. in education and he his M.D. in dental surgery. After their marriage, he developed a fixation with pornography in the so-called men's entertainment magazines. He left the magazines around the house and their relationship deteriorated. Everything he said or did became sexually related, and he suggested that she have sex outside of marriage. He abused his daughter and molested ten of his patients.

Sara was a runaway forced into prostitution. She described how the pimps used pornography to train and hold the girls, and how she tried to escape. "Pornography and prostitution," she said, "are two sides of the same coin."

Kandy described the pornographic aspect of rock music. The basic philosophy of sex in today's rock, she said, is summed up perfectly in Tina Turner's smash hit, "What's Love Got to Do with It?"... "It's only physical...you must try to ignore that it means more than that"... "if it feels good, go for it."

Ingrid asserted that, "You cannot have child pornography without child sexual abuse. They are inseparable." She told about how her father abused her and how she wanted to die because the emotional pain was so great.

Diann described how she was coerced into acting out what her husband had learned from pornography. She told that his entire sex life was based on identity with pornography and on fantasies instead of a real relationship.

Evelyn told how pornography destroyed her happy marriage. Her husband became obsessed with *Playboy,* cheap paperbacks, obscene playing cards, and R-rated movies.

This robbed their children of time and a loving relationship with their father. Her husband wanted her to perform what he saw in pornography, and even progressed to where he wanted to exchange sex partners and participate in orgies.

Brenda told how she became a Playboy Bunny because her father had *Playboy* magazine around the house, and she thought it was acceptable. She told how she and other Playboy Bunnies were depressed and suicidal, and she described the relationship of pornography to suicide, drugs, sex, and VD.

Dr. Frank was the psychiatrist who thoroughly examined a man who committed a brutal rape-murder following nineteen to twenty-four other sexual assaults of women. Dr. Frank described how pornography was an essential part of the criminal's development. He needed pornography to commit sexual assault, and he progressed through every bizarre sex act until the final tragedy.

Susan told how her husband made her perform what he saw in X-rated films, including positions that were painful and caused hemorrhaging. She told how he became sexually abusive after he became a reader of pornography. He told her, "It is supposed to hurt."

James described how he became a victim of pornography starting with crude movies at age twelve. He said that pornography does not stand still, but it feeds on itself and "the decadent becomes more decadent." Now, at age forty-eight with four children, he said, "I still struggle daily with the images, the thoughts, the yearnings, the lusts, cultivated during those years of self-indulgence in pornography." He said that the images are "permanently embedded" in his mind because of the "sticking power" of pornography.

Diana did extensive research on convicted rapists. "Pornography must be understood," she said, "as an important factor contributing to an environment that trivializes, neutralizes, and ultimately facilitates rape."

Dan was introduced to pornography at age nine by a man in his twenties who showed him cartoons with explicit sex acts. He admitted that he has been a "porn addict" for more than forty years, even though he is now a successful professional man, a management-level employee in a large corporation, married and with a family. He recognizes his problem, has had counseling, but the urge never leaves him because he is "held in bondage to pornography."

Diane told how her son Troy died from imitating the autoerotic asphyxiation graphically depicted in an article in *Hustler* magazine called "Orgasm of Death." She found the magazine at her son's feet; it directly caused his death.

Garrett told how, at age ten, a trusted friend of her family and highly respected lawyer sexually abused her, starting with showing her *Playboy* and *Penthouse*. He robbed her of her childhood, and she attempted suicide. Too scared to tell her parents, she confided in the family doctor, and he used the opportunity to assault and abuse her for two more years.

Another woman told how a local cable television company came into town with its package of programming, and her husband became addicted to porn movies within three months. This completely changed their relationship and destroyed their thirty-year marriage. He wanted her to perform the acts he saw in the pornography and, when she wouldn't, he found a woman who would.

These testimonies prove that pornography is addictive, and that those who become addicted crave more bizarre and more perverted pornography, and become more callous toward their victims. Pornography changes the perceptions and attitudes of men toward women, individually and collectively, and desensitizes men so that what was once repulsive and unthinkable becomes not only acceptable but desirable. What was once mere fantasy becomes reality. Thus conditioned and stimulated by pornography, the user seeks a victim.

Victims of the social disease called pornography are crying for help, and concerned citizens with compassion must heed those cries.

WHORING IN UTOPIA

Pat Califia

Even people who are supportive of sex workers' rights often assume that prostitution would somehow wither away if women achieved equality with men or industrial capitalism fell on its blemished, bloated face. Whoring, like other deviant and thus "problematic" sexual behaviors, is assumed to be an artifact of sexism, American imperialism, racism, insane narcotics laws, Christianity, or whatever institutionalized inequity has the pontificator's knickers in a twist.

While large and sweeping social change would probably alter the nature of sex work, the demographics of sex workers, and the wage scale—along with every other kind of human intimacy—I doubt very much that a just society would (or could) eliminate paying for pleasure. Prostitutes, both male and female, have been with us from the earliest recorded time. The "art of prostitution" and "the cult prostitute" are two of the *me* (sacred treasures) given to the Sumerian goddess Inanna by her father Enki, the god of wisdom. When she takes the *me* back to the city of Uruk in the Boat of Heaven, the people turn out in droves to cheer in gratitude. A hymn to Inanna, which describes the people of Sumer parading before her—says: "The male prostitutes comb their hair before you. They decorate the napes of their necks with colored scarves. They drape the cloak of the gods about their shoulders." These poems are 5,000 years old. In fact, Sumer is the first civilization from which we have written texts. There's no reason (other than a certain wistful prudishness) to think that commerce and sex won't continue to intersect as long as either has meaning or a place in human culture.

In America today, the sex industry is shaped by several negative forces. First of all, because the work itself is illegal or plays pretty close to the edge, it attracts people who are desperate, who believe they have few or no other choices, and people who embrace the identity of rebel, outsider, and criminal. Very few sex workers are able to be open with their children, lovers or spouses, friends, and family about what they do for a living. This compartmentalization puts an enormous amount of stress on people who are supposed to get paid for relieving the stress of their customers.

The existence of prostitution as we know it is based on the compartmentalization of male sexuality and female identity. There are women men marry and have children with, and there are women they can screw for a set fee. The wife-and-mother class of women is not supposed to acknowledge the existence of whores, because that would destroy the "good" woman's illusion that *her* faithful, loving husband does not have an alternate identity as a john. The opportunity for paid infidelity (as long as it is hidden and stigmatized) makes monogamous marriage a credible institution. Of course, not every married man has sex with hookers, but enough of them do to keep the black-market economy of sex booming.

The illicit-sex trade interacts and overlaps with other underground economies such as stolen merchandise and smuggling of illegal aliens. But the most influential business is the trade in narcotics. Street prostitution is the only way that most female (and more than a few male) junkies can make enough money to support addiction to the overpriced, adulterated narcotics that our "just say no" social policy on drugs has caused to flood the urban environment. As technology grows more complex and educational opportunities for workers contract, prostitution has become one of the few forms of employment for unskilled laborers. (Another slot for unskilled laborers, which is generated by laws against solicitation, is the vice squad. Cops are often the socioeconomic counterparts of the people they harass, blackmail, bust, and control.)

So what would happen to the sex industry if some of these shaping constraints were lifted? What if narcotics were decriminalized and addicts were able to get prescriptions filled for maintenance doses of good drugs at decent prices? What if prostitution itself were decriminalized *and* destigmatized? If women had the same buying power that men do? If racism no longer forced so many nonwhite citizens into second-class citizenship and poverty? If the virgin/whore dichotomy and the double standard melted away? If everybody had sex education, access to contraception and safe-sex prophylactics, and we no longer believed that sex was toxic? Then wouldn't the free citizens of this wonderful society be able to get all the sex they wanted from other free agents?

Of course not! One of the dominant myths of our culture is that everybody longs to participate in romantic heterosexual love; that it is romance which gives life meaning and purpose; and sex is better when you do it with somebody you love. We are also taught to assume that romance and money are mutually exclusive, even though the heroes of romance novels and neogothics are almost always as wealthy as they are handsome. It would be foolish to deny the existence of romantic passion and lust; but it would be equally foolish to ignore the people who prefer to fuck as far away from the trappings of Valentine's Day as possible. These people don't enjoy the roller coaster ride of romantic love. And there will always be people who simply don't get turned on in the context of an ongoing, committed relationship. Some of these people make trustworthy and affectionate partners as long as you don't expect them to radiate a lot of sexual heat. In a more sex-positive society, these folks might be able to have both marriage and paid sex, without the guilt and stigma of being diagnosed as psychologically "immature" or "incomplete."

It is also possible that prostitution will become romanticized and idealized. The relatively new reality of women as wage earners has generated enormous tension in heterosexual relationships. This hostility has been exacerbated by divorce laws which force men to pay child support and alimony while depriving them of their homes and custody of their children. In a world of prenuptial agreements and lawsuits for breach of promise and sexual harassment, the "good" woman who was once valorized as a suitable candidate for marriage and motherhood is increasingly perceived as a leech and liability. More men may come to feel that "nice girls" are revolted by sex and take all your money, while "fallen women" like cock, like sex, and only want $100 or so. The current media obsession with supermodels needs only a little push to turn it into an image blitz popularizing glamorous courtesans and hookers with hearts of gold and ever-available cunts-without-commitment.

Even in a just society, there would probably be plenty of people who were simply too busy to engage in the ritual of courtship, dating, and seduction. For example, if you have a job that requires you to travel a great deal, you may not have a stable-enough living situation to connect with and keep a steady lover or spouse. Some of these harried businesspeople will be women. Today, male sex workers (whether they identify as gay or straight) service an overwhelmingly male market. I can't imagine what would stop women who can afford it from beckoning the prettiest boys that money can buy to their executive limos, helicopters, and hotel suites. This new job market would have a tremendous impact on the parameters of male heterosexuality, identity, and fashion. Straight men are currently defined mostly by the things that they do not do (wear dresses, get fucked, suck dick, wear bright colors). But in a buyer's market, assertive behavior is at a premium. Female customers will prefer to be serviced by men who actively demonstrate their ability to please women and arousal at the thought of doing so. The word "slut" would lose its gender.

There will always be people who don't have the charm or the social skills to woo a partner. In a society where mutual attraction and sexual reciprocity are the normal basis for bonding, what happens to the people who are not attractive or are unable to or uninterested in giving as good as they get? Disabled people, folks with chronic or terminal illnesses, the elderly, and the sexually dysfunctional will continue to benefit (as they do now) from the ministrations of skilled sex workers who do not discriminate against these populations.

The requirements of fetishists can be very specific. People who have a strong preference for a specific object, act, substance, or physical type will probably continue to find it easier to meet their sexual needs by hiring a professional who has the appropriate wardrobe or toolbox of paraphernalia. Many fetishistic scripts are simply elaborate forms of sublimated and displaced masturbation that do not offer anything other than vicarious pleasure to the fetishist's partner. For example, a shoe fetishist's girlfriend may not be particularly upset about his or her need to be kicked with white patent leather pumps with thirteen straps and an eight-inch heel; but performing this act is probably not going to make her come. Even in utopia, there is no reason for someone to play the martyr and try to be sexually satisfied by an act of charity. Cash evens the bargain and keeps the fetishist from becoming an erotic welfare case. Furthermore, a great many prostitutes' customers have a fetish for paying for sex. It's the sight of that cash sliding into a bustier or a stocking top that makes their dicks get hard, not the cleavage or the shapely thigh.

The first experience one has with physical pleasure has a dramatic impact on the rest of one's life as a sexually active being. In a better world, virgins and novices would probably resort to prostitutes who specialize in rituals of initiation and education. A talented sex worker could introduce brand-new players to all of their sexual options, show them the appropriate way to protect themselves from conception or disease, and teach them the skills they need to please more-experienced partners. This is a sensible antidote to the traumatic rite of passage that "losing your cherry" often is today.

An encounter with a hooker is already a traditional part of bachelor parties. The groom must pay tribute to the Wild Woman and subsidize her freedom before he is allowed to lay claim to a bride he can domesticate. If whoring were not stigmatized, it could be used to celebrate all kinds of holidays. A visit with an especially desirable and skilled sex worker would probably make a great gift for Grandma when she comes out of mourning for her deceased husband. A pregnant wife could thank her husband for being supportive and patient by giving him a weekend with the girl or boy of his dreams. Paid vacations could include sexual services. Bar mitzvahs and other puberty rites would be obvious choices for incorporating orgasms-for-hire, to mark the transition into adulthood.

Since human beings are a curious species, and many of us have a high need for adventure, risk, and excitement, I would hope that the sex industry would continue to be available to fulfill those needs in positive ways. The thrill of arranging several sexual encounters with people you don't know very well certainly seems healthier to me than big-game hunting or full-contact sports, which are high-risk activities sanctioned by our society. The story of the hero who meets a beautiful stranger and wins her favors is archetypal. If we are fortunate, we encounter the anima/animus in our beloved. But until that magical moment, those of us who require refreshment, insight, and sexual nourishment could pay for receiving the blessing. We may have an innate human need to take that mystical journey of transformation into a stranger's arms.

Perhaps sex work will even find its spirituality restored. Those who wish to worship icons of womanhood, manhood, or intersexuality could perform these sacred obligations with sex workers who were guardians of the mysteries of the human heart and loins. The Great Rite, the ancient sacred marriage between earth and sky, teaches us to respect the ecology of the natural world. Perhaps the Sierra Club will begin to sponsor an annual *hieros gamos* as part of its major fund-raising drive. The performers in such a majestic pageant would have to be compensated for their efforts.

It is obvious that, in a kinder, gentler world, the people who sought out sex-for-money would change dramatically. But what about the people who would perform sex work? I wonder whether the boundaries between whore and client might not become more permeable. The prostitute's identity is currently a rather rigid one, partly because once you have been "soiled" by that work, you are never supposed to be able to escape the stigma, but also to create more clarity for the heterosexual male. He is what the prostitute is not: male, moneyed, in charge, legitimate, normal. In a world where women were as likely to be clients as men, sex workers were well paid and in charge of their own lives, and being a prostitute was as valid a social identity as majority whip of the Senate, there would be less need for these high walls between "good" and "bad" people, "men" and "women." Everybody might be expected to spend a portion of their life as a sex worker before getting married, if they didn't want to be thought of as sexually gauche. Perhaps there would be collective brothels where people could perform community service to work off parking tickets or student loans. A stint in the community pleasure house might be analogous to going on retreat.

The people who took up sex work as a profession would be more likely to feel a vocation for the erotic arts, just as priests or artists do today for their professions. They would be teachers, healers, adventurous souls, tolerant and compassionate. Prostitutes are all of those things today, but they perform their acts of kindness and virtue in an ungrateful milieu. The profession would attract people who like to work for themselves, who are bored easily, who want a lot of social contact and stimulation. It would also attract people who are dramatic, exhibitionistic performers and storytellers. As computer technology is used for sexual purposes, sex workers will need to be computer literate. The ideal sex worker might be somebody who is skilled at creating virtual realities, programming environments, characters, plots, and sensations for the client. This programming ability might become more compellingly sexy than a pair of big tits or a ten-inch dick.

Sex work would also attract stone butches of both sexes and all sexual orientations—people who want to run the fuck, but are not very interested in experiencing their own sexual vulnerability and pleasure. Often these sorts of people are the most adept at manipulating other people's experiences. They are more objective about their partners' fantasies and do not become distracted by their own needs, since their need is to remain remote and in control.

There are other social changes which will continue to alter the dynamics of the sex industry. In a society where everybody was doing work they enjoyed for a fair wage, the meaning of money (and work itself) would change. It would cease to be a sex marker, for one thing (I am male, so I earn a paycheck; you are female, so men give you money). This change is already under way. In a postindustrial society where power was cheap or free and survival was no longer an issue, money might even cease to be a marker for social class. I believe that human beings will still have a need to group themselves into smaller tribes or social units based on affinity and common interests. People will have new and unforeseen ecological slots as "the one who pays/gives" or "the one who gets paid/receives" for possessing certain characteristics or performing different activities.

Unfortunately, it's doubtful that any of these visions will be realized. As AIDS paranoia grows and nation-states continue to consolidate and extend their power, it is much more likely that sex workers will face harsher penalties and stepped-up law-enforcement campaigns. In a few radical locales, prostitution might be legalized and subjected to strict government regulation as a social experiment to control AIDS and other sexually transmitted diseases. People seem to be suckers for anything, whether it's motorcycle helmet laws or the Brady bill, which promises to make us safer. There is really no guarantee that making the federal government the greatest pimp of all would do a goddamned thing to make sex work a better career or protect the health and safety of the customer. In a system like this, prostitutes would be like mill workers in late-nineteenth-century

England. But a state that believes it has the right to send young men off to die in a war or conduct above-ground testing of atomic weapons in populated areas is eventually going to try to take over the hands, mouths, dicks, cunts, and buttholes which are sex workers' means of production. So the halcyon, golden days of prostitution may be happening tight now. This may be as good, liberal, and free as it gets. So you might want to visit your ATM, take out a couple of hundred bucks, and hurry to the red-light district now, before it becomes as antiquated as a Wild West ghost town.

ABOUT THE AUTHORS

Michael C. Botkin is a San Francisco Queer activist, regular columnist for the city's queer *Bay Area Reporter,* and "Sleazy Editrix" of *Diseased Pariah News,* The HIVer humor 'Zine.

Jim Bramlett is a full-time volunteer for Campus Crusade for Christ at its World Headquarters in Orlando, Florida.

A book of **Pat Califia**'s essays on sexuality will be published by Cleis Press next year. Her most recent books are a collection of short erotic fiction (Melting Point, Alyson Publications, 1993) and a handbook for couples exploring S/M (Sensuous Magic, Masquerade Books, 1993). She has worked in the sex industry as a professional dominatrix and a porn model.

Joseph P. Cunningham's column "Fighting Back" appears in *Penthouse.* He is currently working on a book about censorship and a graphic novel, *Dystopia.*

Cecil E. Greek is Assistant Professor of Criminology at the University of South Florida. *Porn Wars: A comparison of American and British Anti-pornography Campaigns in the 1980s,* co-authored with William Thompson, will be published by Aldine de Gruyter in 1994.

Mark Kramer is a New York-based investigative hack who has written for *Screw, The Realist, CrimeBeat, National Enquirer* and *The Weekly World News.*

Ron Leming is a well-known, highly respected artist in the small press.

Stan Leventhal is the author of numerous books including *Mountain Climbing in Sheridan Square, A Herd of Tiny Elephants,* and *Candy Holidays.*

Bobby Lilly is the founder and chairperson of Californians Against Censorship Together (CAL-ACT).

Andy Mangels is a mainstream comic-book writer whose work includes *Nightmare on Elm Street* and upcoming issues of *Quantum Leap* and the *Batman Adventures*. He is the editor of *Gay Comics*.

Michael Medved is co-host of *Sneak Previews* on PBS and film critic for the *New York Post*. He is also the author of *Hollywood vs. America* and six other nonfiction books.

William Relling, Jr. makes his third appearance in *Gauntlet* with this interview. His short fiction, censored by various publishers, has appeared in issues #1 and #2.

Stephen R. Rohde, a graduate of Northwestern University and Columbia Law School, practices constitutional law in Los Angeles. The author of numerous articles and a frequent lecturer on the First Amendment, Mr. Rohde is Co-Chair of the Los Angeles County Bar Association Committee on the Bicentennial of the Bill of Rights. His most recent work, "Art of the State: Congressional Censorship of the National Endowment for the Arts," was published by the *Hastings Communication and Entertainment Law Journal* (Vol. 12, No. 3 p.353).

Phyllis Schlafly is the author of thirteen books and the president of Eagle Forum.

Don Vaughan is a freelance writer and journalist from Florida.

Wally Wharton, the self-proclaimed "Thinking Man's Bimbo," has a monthly column in *Hustler's Erotic Video Guide* titled "Wally's Whack World!" Often referred to as a female Will Rogers in latex, Wharton is also the author of a humor book that needs a publisher with the balls to take on *Dating for Dollars—A Girl's Guide to Greed*.

Kate Worley has been the writer of *Omaha the Cat Dancer* since 1986. She wears her "I write banned books" button with pride.

BIZARRE SEX

BIZARRE SEX AND OTHER CRIMES OF PASSION

Edited by Stan Tal

Stan Tal, editor of *Bizarre Sex*, Canada's boldest fiction publication, has culled the very best stories that have crossed his desk—and now unleashes them on the reading public in ***Bizarre Sex and Other Crimes of Passion***. Over twenty small masterpieces of erotic shock make this one of the year's most unexpectedly alluring anthologies. Including such masters of erotic horror and fantasy as Edward Lee, Lucy Taylor, Nancy Kilpatrick and Caro Soles, ***Bizarre Sex***, is a treasure-trove of arousing chills. ***213-2/$12.95***

LUCY TAYLOR

UNNATURAL ACTS

A remarkable debut volume from a provocative writer. ***Unnatural Acts*** plunges deep into the dark side of the psyche, far past all pleasantries and prohibitions, and brings to life a disturbing vision of erotic horror. Unrelenting angels and hungry gods play with souls and bodies in Taylor's murky cosmos: where heaven and hell are mere differences of perspective; where redemption and damnation lie behind the same shocking acts. ***181-0/$12.95***

PAT CALIFIA

SENSUOUS MAGIC

Renowned erotic pioneer Pat Califia provides this honest, unpretentious peek behind the mask of dominant/submissive sexuality—an adventurous adult world of pleasure too often obscured by ignorance and fear. With her trademark wit and insight, Califia demystifies "the scene" for the novice, explaining the terminology and technique behind many misunderstood sexual practices The adventurous (or just plain curious) lover won't want to miss this ultimate "how to" volume. ***131-4/$12.95***

JOHN PRESTON

MY LIFE AS A PORNOGRAPHER

& Other Indecent Acts

Unlike most "experts" who purport to discuss pornography, John Preston writes with authority and authenticity. No self-styled victim or "objective" voyeur, this is a man who has dared to explore his own pornographic imagination to the fullest. Some of the essays here are as intimate as pornography itself, addressed to a circle of initiates. Others—like the famous reply to Sally Gearhart, the ode to Sam Steward, the landmark Harvard lecture—have had a much wider impact. In a reflective mood, Preston ends with a "Modest Proposal" for the support of pornography, and no sager or more succinct words of advice on the subject could be found than in the book's very last sentence.

—Steven Saylor (Aaron Travis)

"...essential and enlightening...His sex-positive stand on safer-sex education as the only truly effective AIDS-prevention strategy will certainly not win him any conservative converts, but AIDS activists will be shouting their assent.... ***[My Life as a Pornographer]*** *is a bridge from the sexually liberated 1970s to the more cautious 1990s, and Preston has walked much of that way as a standard-bearer to the cause for equal rights...."*

—Library Journal

135-7/$12.95

HUSTLING:

A Gentleman's Guide to the Fine Art of Homosexual Prostitution

...valuable insights to many aspects of the world of gay male prostitution. Throughout the book, Preston uses materials gathered from interviews and letters from former and active hustlers, as well as insights gleaned from his own experience as a hustler.... Preston does fulfill his desire to entertain as well as educate.

—Lambda Book Report

The very first guide to the gay world's most infamous profession. John Preston solicited the advice and opinions of "working boys" from across the country in his effort to produce the ultimate guide to the hustler's world. ***Hustling*** covers every practical aspect of the business, from clientele and payment options to "specialties", sidelines and drawbacks. No stone is left unturned—and no wrong turn left unadmonished—in this guidebook to the ins and outs of this much-mythologized trade. ***137-3/$12.95***

CARO SOLES

MELTDOWN!

An Anthology of Erotic Science Fiction and Dark Fantasy for Gay Men

Editor Caro Soles has put together one of the most explosive, mind-bending collections of gay erotic writing ever published. ***Meltdown!*** contains the very best examples of this increasingly popular sub-genre of explicit fiction: stories meant to shock and delight, to send a shiver down the spine and start a fire down below. A volume of extraordinary imagination, ***Meltdown!*** presents both new voices and provocative pieces by world-famous novelists Edmund White and Samuel R. Delany. ***203-5/$12.95***

SKINTWO

THE BEST OF *SKIN TWO* ***Edited by Tim Woodward***

For over a decade, *Skin Two* has served as the bible of the international fetish community. A groundbreaking journal from the crossroads of sexuality, fashion, and art, *Skin Two* specializes in provocative, challenging essays by the finest writers working in the "radical sex" scene. Collected here, for the first time, are the articles and interviews that have established the magazine's singular reputation. ***130-6/$12.95***

MARCO VASSI

THE STONED APOCALYPSE

"...Marco Vassi is our champion sexual energist."—VLS

During his lifetime, Marco Vassi was hailed as America's premier erotic writer and most worthy successor to Henry Miller. His work was praised by writers as diverse as Gore Vidal and Norman Mailer, and his reputation was worldwide. ***The Stoned Apocalypse*** is Vassi's autobiography, financed by the other groundbreaking erotic writing that made him a cult sensation. Chronicling a cross-country trip on America's erotic byways, it offers a rare glimpse of a generation's sexual imagination. ***132-2/$12.95***

A DRIVING PASSION

"Let me leave you with A Driving Passion. It is, in effect, an introduction and overview of all his other books, and my hope is that it will lead readers to explore the bold literary contribution of Marco Vassi."

—Norman Mailer

While he was primarily known and respected as a novelist, Vassi was also an effective and compelling speaker. ***A Driving Passion*** collects the wit and insight Vassi brought to his lectures, and distills the philosophy—including the concept of Metasex—that made him an underground sensation. An essential volume. ***134-9/$12.95***

THE EROTIC COMEDIES

A collection of stories from America's premier erotic philosopher. Marco Vassi was a dedicated iconoclast, and ***The Erotic Comedies*** marked a high point in his literary career. Scathing and humorous, these stories reflect Vassi's belief in the power and primacy of Eros in American life, as well as his commitment to the elimination of personal repression through carnal indulgence. A wry collection for the sexually adventurous. ***136-5/$12.95***

THE SALINE SOLUTION

During the Sexual Revolution, Marco Vassi established himself as an intrepid explorer of an uncharted sexual landscape. During this time he also distinguished himself as a novelist, producing ***The Saline Solution*** to great acclaim. With the story of one couple's brief affair and the events that lead them to desperately reassess their lives, Vassi examines the dangers of intimacy in an age of extraordinary freedom. A remarkably clear-eyed look at the growing pains of a generation. ***180-2/$12.95***